KAVITA DASWANI is an international journalist covering fashion, beauty, travel, design and celebrities for a range of global publications. A former fashion editor for the *South China Morning Post* in Hong Kong and Asian correspondent for *WWD*, for whom she still writes, she currently contributes to the *Los Angeles Times*, *Cosmetic News Weekly*, *Tatler*, *Crave* and numerous other publications.

She has also written for the Indian editions of *Vogue*, *Condé Nast Traveller* and *Grazia Italia*.

She lives in Los Angeles with her husband and two sons. She has authored the best-selling books *For Matrimonial Purposes*, *The Village Bride of Beverly Hills*, *Indie Girl* and *Salaam, Paris*. Her books have been published in seventeen languages.

BOMBAY GIRL

Kavita Daswani

HarperCollins *Publishers* India
a joint venture with

New Delhi

First published in India in 2012 by
HarperCollins *Publishers* India
a joint venture with
The India Today Group

ISBN: 978-93-5029-329-4

2 4 6 8 10 9 7 5 3 1

Kavita Daswani asserts the moral right to be identified
as the author of this work.

This is a work of fiction and all characters and incidents described in this book
are the product of the author's imagination. Any resemblance to actual persons,
living or dead, is entirely coincidental.

HarperCollins *Publishers*
A-53, Sector 57, Noida, Uttar Pradesh 201301, India
77-85 Fulham Palace Road, London W6 8JB, United Kingdom
Hazelton Lanes, 55 Avenue Road, Suite 2900, Toronto, Ontario M5R 3L2
and 1995 Markham Road, Scarborough, Ontario M1B 5M8, Canada
25 Ryde Road, Pymble, Sydney, NSW 2073, Australia
31 View Road, Glenfield, Auckland 10, New Zealand
10 East 53rd Street, New York NY 10022, USA

Typeset in ITC Giovanni Std 10.5/14
InoSoft Systems Noida

Printed and bound at
Manipal Technologies Ltd., Manipal

For Mummy and Papa,
whose love wrote the story of my life

PART ONE

the bottom of a generic plastic tray. I felt a lurch in my stomach. Tears sprung up in my eyes.

Jag had walked out on me six days ago. As much as he had claimed to love me, in the end he couldn't get far enough away from who I was. He had said I belonged to the wrong family, that he had discovered there was bad blood between his family and mine. That it could never work, that we could not survive without the blessings of our parents. I told him I would walk away from the life I had known, that I would leave my family to be with him, that he was the only man I'd ever loved. I would have done anything.

It didn't matter how much I pled. He left anyway. After two glorious months together, capped by a commitment in the form of this wispy chain affixed with a sapphire peace emblem, he had left. He would not be coming back.

And now, here I was, about to board a flight from London back to my home in Mumbai, to the comforting arms of my family, the same family that had, in some way unbeknownst to me, precipitated the loss of the best man I had ever known and hoped to make mine.

I made it through security check. I threw the chain into the bottom of my bag and hurried to catch my flight.

PROLOGUE

The queue in front of me moved slowly, everyone pausing to toss belts, phones, keys and coins into plastic trays. Overhead, a voice on the loudspeaker called out to wayward passengers to rush to their gates. Heathrow is a very easy airport to lose oneself in.

I walked through the metal detector. A faint beep went off. A red light.

'Miss, can you remove all your jewellery, please?' I turned towards the security officer, a big-hipped woman with tightly curled brown hair. She was eyeing my chain. I raised my hand to it, fumbled for the clasp, unhooked it and tossed it into the tray, where it lay sadly in a corner. It hadn't left my neck since it was given to me a few weeks ago when Jag had put it on me, in the middle of *The X Factor*, me in my frog-print flannel pyjamas. He had said to me, 'Wear it always.' I promised I would.

I looked at it now, small, lost and curled up in

ONE

Around the same time every morning, Chanoo slipped out of the house, strolled to the corner news stand and purchased the day's newspapers – the *Times of India*, the *Economic Times*, *Mint*. As the household's head servant, she had earned the privilege of a few moments of respite in a day otherwise crowded with more strenuous domestic chores.

As she always did, she brought the papers to my parents' bedroom, alongside a tray holding a steaming cup of tea and a small glass jar of honey soaked almonds, my mother's morning staple.

My father had just left for work, and I took advantage of his absence from my parents' room to join my mother there, where I lay on her warm bed, immersed in Jane Austen. I was still healing from my break-up with Jag, still reeling from the bitter disappointment of it, trying to figure out what had gone wrong. I asked questions of my family that nobody would answer.

My mother settled into an armchair and arranged the newspapers on a small table in front of her, leaving them crisp and pristine for later on, when my father would come home for lunch and catch up on his reading.

But something on the front page of the *Daily Business Journal*, the country's leading financial newspaper, caught her eye.

'What is this?' she asked, frowning.

I set my book down and walked over to my mother's side. On the front page was a photograph of my grandfather and his three sons. The headline read: 'Who are the Badshahs?', and below that, 'How This Family Came Out of Nowhere to Claw its Way to the Top'.

'This is not possible,' Mom said. 'This is a mistake. A joke.'

Seeing my grandfather, father and two uncles on the cover of a leading daily newspaper felt incongruous, phony, and my initial thought was that it was a gag, one of those fake newspaper front pages you commissioned for a special occasion or a practical joke. I took the paper from my mother's hand and rifled through the pages.

There was a story on the rising power of the rupee, an analysis of the most bullish IPOs, a piece on the technological prowess of Karnataka.

This was no gag. This was real.

Phones were ringing. My mother's mobile, lying on her dressing table, vibrated urgently. Chanoo appeared at the doorway and said that Dad was on the phone in the living room, and wanted to speak to Mom immediately.

'This cannot be,' Mom muttered again, looking vaguely towards me.

I nodded in weak agreement.

But I had an unshakeable feeling that after this day, things would be very different for all of us.

'They kept calling for an interview,' my father said, back home a few hours later. 'We declined. They ran a story anyway.'

'But I don't understand how they got this information,' Mom said. 'They are talking about all this stuff, all this *wealth*, that we … that *you* have, Jeetu,' she lowered her voice. 'Tell me, is it true? Are we really, you know, *this?*'

Dad didn't answer. He shook his head, took another sip of Scotch.

'Baba must be furious,' my mother continued. 'He loves his privacy, his … secrets.'

She was right. My grandfather was a man who loathed the limelight, who thought that overt displays of grandeur were as gross as lovers groping one another in public.

'Dad, how did they find these pictures?' I asked, leaning forward to pick up the newspaper again. 'Where did they get this information?'

'These days, anyone can find out anything,' my father sneered. He stirred the ice cubes in his tumbler with his finger. 'Goddamn journalists.'

I looked at the photo again, a generic corporate shot, taken for the group's internal purposes. Baba was perched on the cognac-coloured leather armchair in his office, a cream-coloured Nehru jacket stretched over his large frame, his full white hair reminiscent of a lion's mane. His interlocked fingers were studded with large rings, a chunky weave of coral and emeralds and rubies, prescribed by various astrologers, and destined to help Baba get, in the words of one, 'from zero to hero.'

My father and his two brothers, one older, one younger, stood around my grandfather, looking homogenous in their dark suits and shiny ties, with side-swept clipped hair and vague smiles.

On an inside page were more pictures: an exterior shot of the squat, grey hued building in central Mumbai that was home to Badshah Industries, the company that Baba had founded fifty years ago; a black-and-white photo of Baba as a young man, his legs scrawny and face solemn, outside a steel mill. The caption read, 'Darshan

Badshah, 20, at his first job'. A montage in a corner showed my aunts and mother at charity events. And, at the bottom, a tiny headshot of me with my best friend Nitya, taken at an art gallery opening. The caption read: 'Sohana Badshah, the lone heiress, currently studying interior design in London.' There was an inaccuracy, right there: I *had* been enrolled in a nine-month interior decorating course, but abandoned it within three months, unable to bear being in London after Jag had left.

'It will be old news tomorrow,' my mother said to Dad, trying to reassure him. 'People will forget about it.'

My father stared blankly at her.

TWO

Alone in my room that night, I turned to the paper again, grateful for the opportunity to read it properly. It was written by Manjuli Khosla, senior financial correspondent. Next to that were the names, penned in tinier print, of four other reporters who had contributed to the story from different cities.

The story began with the headline: 'India's Newest Dynasty', and under that: 'How Did Darshan Badshah Get This Rich?'

I couldn't help but be amused by the ridiculousness of it. Even though it was the *Daily Business Journal*, it felt like pure tabloid nonsense. If Mumbai high society was one raucously privileged frat house, we were still the geeks, the outsiders, perched on a rung – as far as I knew, anyway – significantly lower than everyone else. There were distinctions even among the wealthy. We flew Business, not First, and would never even consider having a private jet, like so many of our acquaintances had. We bought ready-to-wear, not couture. The family car was a Mercedes, not a Rolls, and it was at least five years old. Baba had lived in the same house for decades, comfortable and spacious but not exactly a palace. The information in the article was a revelation to me. Being wealthy was one thing – but our family owning the richest private company in India? Not by a long shot.

But as I skimmed over the columns and boxes packed with facts and figures, I learned things I had never known. In the past couple of years, my family had acquired steel mills in Orissa, turned around a struggling hotel chain in Europe, diversified into liquor and tobacco, purchased vast tracts of arable land in Pondicherry and entire apartment buildings in Manhattan. Whatever they were doing had, according to the story, propelled my family to the top of the list of privately held companies in India.

For five decades, Darshan Badshah has been one of Mumbai's quietly prosperous businessmen and philanthropists, reaping big profits in steel mills, manufacturing and agriculture. He is completely self-made. And during all these years, he has shunned the spotlight, preferring to work behind the scenes.

But he can hide in the shadows no longer. In the past few years, he and his three sons, Amit, Jeetu and Prakash, have steadily reinforced the family coffers, although sometimes through controversial and even questionable means. In 2009, Badshah Exports Ltd, a Hong Kong-based trading company, was accused of manufacturing counterfeit branded sportswear in China for export to Panama. The suit was settled out-of-court for an undisclosed sum. The same year, there were allegations that Badshah Pharmaceuticals in Sion falsified data about the generic drugs it produces for the US market. There is also an ongoing property-related breach of contract case in New Jersey (see below).

My eye went to the bottom right-hand corner. There was a small black-lined box. The top line read: 'Late-breaking news'. Beneath that, two short paragraphs.

A state judge in New Jersey this week ruled in favour of Kismet Corporation in its legal battle with Badshah Inc, the US subsidiary of Badshah Industries, over breach of contract.

According to court documents, Kismet Corporation in 2007 purchased a 200-acre site in Morris County in what was to be a joint-venture deal with Badshah Inc. Badshah was leading a consortium of investors from India who would invest US$150 million to develop a retail and dining complex on the land. In the suit, filed in July 2008, Balu Sachdev, founder of Kismet Corp., alleges that Badshah reneged on its agreement. Lawyers for Badshah said the company would appeal, citing an out clause in the contract allowing for the agreement to be terminated in the event of an economic downturn.

I felt my body turn cold.

This was it. This was why Jag had left me.

Balu Sachdev was his father. *This* was the bad blood.

A lawsuit. A hundred-and-fifty million dollars. A broken promise.

Up until now, we had never given the tabloids any reason to dig. None of the Badshahs had ever had wild extramarital affairs. Our offices hadn't been raided by tax officials. We didn't perversely captivate an entire city for years by building a skyscraping home. But now, seemingly out of nowhere, journalists wanted to know about us. My family – Baba and his three sons – appeared to have done things that warranted attention. And, as unlikely as it appeared, I had been caught in the crosshairs. I tossed the newspaper onto my bed and went to my closet.

I searched in the piles of clothes until I found an ebony lacquered box hidden at the back. Its surface had an engraving of a pair of golden bells strung together with a flowing ribbon.

The box had been a party favour at a wedding I had attended in London, on the night Jag and

I had first met. It had contained a gold-dipped coffee spoon studded with a tiny red crystal, laid on a scarlet satin lining. It was one of the few party souvenirs I had ever preserved because of its association with the man I loved.

I opened it now, and pulled out the other things I kept inside, nesting atop the spoon. A photo of Jag and me, at an impromptu Sunday night dinner at Royal China, one of London's best Chinese eateries. Jag's arm wrapped around the back of my chair, his hair thick and curly, his face open, chin boasting that tiny dimple I loved; me looking bright-eyed, clearly in love.

Coiled up in a corner of the box was the chain he had given me.

Since returning from London, I had spent most of my time trying to understand why our relationship ended. And now, because of a few lines at the bottom of a newspaper report that had unsettled my family, I finally knew at least part of the reasons.

But it left me no better off than before.

THREE

Beyond what it had meant for me, the impact of the story was felt far and wide. It was the top story on Google News, and, for a couple of hours, Badshah was among the most widely trending subjects on Twitter. I couldn't even count the number of messages I had received on my Facebook page.

The switchboard at Badshah Industries was flooded with calls from correspondents at *Forbes* and *Fortune*, *Time* and *Newsweek*. Flowers and gift baskets arrived from all quarters. Long-lost relatives and faraway acquaintances emerged, requesting start-up capital, a loan, a random hospital bill to be paid. With my mother's numerous friends calling to congratulate her, the phone at home didn't stop ringing. She would accept their warm wishes (which she said were generally delivered in rather a sour tone) and then tell them that the dollar amounts quoted in the story were a gross exaggeration.

'How are you feeling about everything?' Milan, my favourite cousin, asked me, stopping by the evening the story appeared. After I had read the entire article, down to the bit about Balu Sachdev and his travails with my family, Milan had been my first call.

'At least I know now that Jag wasn't making it up,' I said. 'But all that stuff about the shadowy things that the family has been up to – I had no idea about any of it. Are we, like, some criminal syndicate or something?'

'No more than any other rich Indian family,' he smiled. 'Nobody comes to this kind of wealth, the kind that Baba has, without being a little shady. I'm loving every minute of it, though. I think I'm going to get a lot more hot-chick action.'

I grinned at my cousin who, a year younger than me, was every inch the self-indulged heir. If he had his way, he'd have 'India's Newest Dynasty' tattooed on his forehead.

'Listen, Soh,' he said, addressing me by my pet name. 'Forget all this dark and depressing stuff. Let's just have some fun with it.'

'What are you talking about?' I asked, about to walk out of the room. He grabbed me by the arm.

'Abandon the whole goody-two-shoes crap for five minutes. Isn't there something you've always wanted to do?'

'Well …' I hesitated.

I had, in truth, been obsessed with a Mughal empress I had seen in a movie, whose signature was to walk into a room and command everyone to disperse. I used to imitate her in front of my mirror, folding my arms in front of me, straightening up and barking out orders to nobody. It filled me with an odd sense of power – a sense that I did not ordinarily possess.

I now made the mistake of telling Milan about this perverse fantasy of mine, and before I knew it, he was shepherding me towards the kitchen. We arrived at the doorway to the kitchen, where Chanoo was giving orders to the cooks for dinner while the kitchen boys were washing the utensils. They all summarily turned to look at us in surprise. The kitchen was not a room I frequented often.

'Ji,' Chanoo said, gazing at me expectantly. 'Kuch chahiye?'

Milan poked his finger into the small of my back.

'Takliya!' I said out loud. They were supposed to scatter, like ants being spritzed with pesticide. But instead they all stood rooted to the spot, expressionless. Chanoo raised a scant eyebrow in my direction.

'Sorry,' I muttered, turning around and leaving. Milan chortled loudly behind me.

'This whole bloody rich-girl gig is wasted on you,' he laughed.

I could not help but agree.

FOUR

Every alternate Friday, we gathered at Baba's Malabar Hill home for dinner. It was an enduring family tradition. We were expected to be there, unless we had a perfectly sound reason not to be present. Apart from two occasions when I'd had the flu, and those three months that I'd spent in London, I hadn't missed dinner at Baba's in years. All my cousins complained about it, but I almost enjoyed it. Even though Baba barely spoke to me, he always seemed genuinely happy to see me.

By the time I arrived with my parents and younger brother Rajan who, at thirteen, was the baby of the family, my cousins were already assembled: Sharan was in the veranda, Bluetooth in ear, in heated discussion with some faraway associate. He was the eldest grandchild, the first son of Baba's first son Amit, and as a consequence, the most likely to eventually head the business. Sharan had a younger brother Karan who also

worked at Badshah and was in Dubai that night,
overseeing the construction of luxury villas which
Badshah would turn around and sell. Milan and
his twin brother Pawan, the sons of my dad's
younger brother Prakash, were engrossed in a
video game on the big-screen TV, their long legs
stretched out on the coffee table. Rajan rushed
over to join them.

My older brother, Armaan, an art director with
his own business, was off on a photo shoot. This
was the third consecutive Friday night gathering
he had missed. I knew that Baba would be
keeping track.

My mother adjourned to a corner with Amit
Uncle's wife Malini, and Prakash Chacha's wife
Preeti. Malini was flashy, shiny, big-haired and
favoured shimmery leopard-print dresses. Preeti
had a naughty sense of humour, a laugh that
filled the room and a love of Tru Religion jeans.
She had captivated Prakash Chacha with her pale
green eyes and calm authenticity.

My mother was somewhere in the middle. Like
Malini, she preferred her diamonds flawless, but
she also had a lot of Preeti's earthiness. She was a
grounded, genuine woman, not easily swayed by
silly social dictates. They were joined by Sharan's
wife Jaanvi, who came in and touched the feet
of the elders, like the dutiful daughter-in-law

she was. Sharan, still in the veranda, ignored his wife's arrival.

Across the room, my father and his brothers sat around a small cherrywood cocktail table, tossing roasted chickpeas into their mouths. They said very little to each other, which was not terribly surprising given that they had spent all day together at the office. I went up to say hello to them; I especially loved Amit Uncle who treated me as his daughter. He used to play practical jokes on his younger siblings when they were children, and some of that mischief still lurked in his eyes. He put his arm around me and pulled me down onto the seat next to him.

'What kind of fun have you been having lately?' he asked, pinching my cheek like I was five. He was the sort of uncle who would routinely shoot down a family member's suggestion that I marry this boy or that, insisting that I was far too good for those suitors. Then he would wink at me, tell me to find a real man on my own, one who would know how to truly care for me. He would have loved Jag.

The large double doors leading to the hall opened, and Baba walked in, his wife, Dadi, by his side. Everyone stood up instantly, Milan and Pawan letting their gaming consoles clatter to the floor, Sharan quickly ending his conversation, pressing his earpiece and pocketing it.

Baba glanced around the room, as if taking a mental inventory of who had bothered to come, and vaguely nodded his approval. He turned his eyes my way and marched towards me. I stiffened. He was standing a mere couple of inches from me, his bushy eyebrows knitted together in a frown. My hand tightened around a glass of chilled orange juice. He cupped my spare hand in his. 'Sohana Beta, how are you? Looking pretty today,' he said.

I bowed my head deferentially, as if he were a king and I a menial pageboy. Baba dropped my hand as abruptly as he had taken hold of it, turned, and strolled out of the room and across the hallway to the dining room, tacitly commanding all of us to follow.

'Looking pretty today,' said Milan, coming up behind me, imitating Baba's gravelly voice. 'Shit, yaar, what does a guy have to do to get a little love around here? Become a girl?'

'Shut up,' I said. 'I am the *only* girl, you know.'

'Yes, Soh, this is something you seem to never let us forget.'

He put his arm through mine and we crossed the hallway. At the entrance to the dining room, one of the servants held out an engraved silver bowl, into which we all knew to deposit our mobiles, Blackberries, iPhones and any other gadgets we had in our pockets and purses. Baba was adamant that there be no high-tech intrusions at the table, that we were all to eat and, hopefully, even converse with one another, and not succumb to the constant lure of communicating with people beyond those walls.

Sharan reluctantly threw his Bluetooth into the bowl, where it let out a tinny clatter as it hit the bottom. He rolled his eyes, indicating his displeasure at the enforced confiscation.

I took my usual seat at the far end of the table, close to my cousins, and opposite Baba who sat at the head with Dadi on his right. Baba's chair had a high, straight back, longer than those on the rest of the dining chairs, and so imposing that it felt more like a throne, a throwback to some majestic Mughal period. The part of the back that faced outwards had a dramatic relief sculpture carved onto the wood – the face of a fanged lion, its nostrils flared, hand-painted gold and red. Anywhere else, it would be tacky, a Las Vegas showpiece. But, given the nature of the man who occupied it – a proud Leo – it was a fitting piece of furniture.

The table had been custom-made for Baba. It was long, with the edges sharp at one end, curved at the other – an architectural anomaly. But Baba had requested it to be built that way, so that there would only be one true 'head', and a few of us would have to cluster around the curve of the opposite end.

At the table, much like in life, Baba could have no equal.

The servants sprang to life the second we were all seated, ferrying platters of food to the table, pouring glasses of lemon juice, iced water, whisky, entering and leaving the adjacent kitchen as if it were rush hour in a restaurant. The only sound to be heard was that of cutlery scraping across plates. Nobody was uttering a word.

'Baba, you are looking well,' my mother said brightly, always the one to try and liven things up. 'Have you been going for your morning walk?'

Baba grunted in acknowledgement, readjusted the napkin into his collar and continued eating. Milan looked at me; I knew he wanted to ask Baba about the newspaper report. We hadn't seen Baba since the story had come out. But Milan held himself back. My aunts twittered about some saris they had seen that afternoon, and Pawan and Rajan discussed the merits of Red Dead Redemption. I glanced around the table and saw my relatives straining to make conversation. The atmosphere seemed stifled, stressed.

Baba stopped eating and yanked his napkin out of his shirt, indicating that dinner was officially over. I hurriedly shoved the final pieces of curried mutton into my mouth. Baba stood up and turned, about to walk out of the room. He stopped, and swivelled back slowly.

'I know you are all waiting for me to say something about that very distasteful story,' he said in his low growl of a voice. 'I will only say this, and then I want to hear nothing more about it.' He paused for effect. He had the gravitas of Laurence Olivier.

'The article changes nothing. We will continue to be a private family. We will continue to keep our personal lives to ourselves. Does everyone understand?'

All of us nodded obediently, except Milan, who stared defiantly at Baba.

I felt a flutter in my stomach. There was something that needed to be asked. Nobody else seemed to be asking it. Everyone was hoping that the elephant in the room would keel over and die. But I knew better.

I trembled. This was not an open forum. But I had to ask.

'Baba?' I said, in a small voice.

He looked at me.

'Yes?'

'Is it true?'

'What?' He was frowning at me, those silvery caterpillar brows hidden under a mound of creases.

'The article. Is it true?'

I waited for him to bellow, the way I had heard him so many times before – at his sons, his daughters-in-law, his servants. At all of us. He shouted at everyone except his wife. And, oddly, at me.

'What does it matter?' he replied.

I didn't pursue the conversation.

'But,' he said, bearing his knuckles down onto his place mat, 'we have something urgent to attend to.'

He turned towards my father and uncles. 'You three know what I'm talking about,' he said. His voice was cold. 'That … that *bullshit* in the newspaper has proved the necessity of it. A decision has to be made. Soon.'

Milan and I looked at each other, mystified.

Dadi glanced sideways at her husband, a look of mild disapproval fleeting across her face. Everyone was quiet. Baba turned around to leave.

And with that, he stalked out of the room, Dadi following in his wake.

FIVE

We remained at the table, too stunned to move.

'Dude! What was *that*?' said Milan. 'What's the old man talking about?'

Dad and his brothers were stony in their silence.

'This isn't the time to discuss it,' said Amit Uncle. 'Baba is upset about certain things.'

The cousins all glanced at me.

'What?' I asked.

'Yeah, Soh, must be you,' said Milan, half-joking. 'Twenty-six and no husband. You're practically a relic.'

I threw my napkin at him.

'It's not her,' my father said quietly.

Heads turned, almost in unison, towards Sharan and Jaanvi. They had been married for three years and there was still no baby. For now, the responsibility of the creation of another generation rested solely on Jaanvi's lacklustre womb. She had been hand-picked by Sharan's parents more for her pedigree than anything else. Milan called her 'The Dud'. Now, in addition to her deficiency in the looks-and-personality department, it seemed she couldn't produce an heir.

Jaanvi sat back in her chair, her arms defensively folded across her chest.

'We are trying,' she said quietly, reading everyone's mind. Sharan squirmed next to her, looking decidedly emasculated. 'Does anyone want more food or shall I call the servants to clear the table?'

In the car on the way home, my father, seated in the front, next to the driver, appeared to be deep in thought. I was squeezed in the back between my mother who reeked of Estée Lauder Youth Dew, and Rajan, the vague buzz of a hip-hop tune emanating from his iPod. I turned to look out of the window as we made our way down the streets of Mumbai to our apartment on Nepean Sea Road.

'What did he mean, Dad?' I said. 'What was Baba talking about?'

My father shot a knowing glance at my mother. They wouldn't tell me anything, firstly because they still saw me as a child, and secondly because they knew never to speak of anything remotely private in front of the driver, whose nickname of 'The Informant' among our servants was not entirely unjustified.

'We will talk later,' my father replied tersely, ending the matter.

By the time we got home, my older brother Armaan was in his room, downloading images onto his computer. His shirt smelled like it had been doused in tobacco juice.

I had not seen him in a couple of days; he had been shooting an ad campaign for a new vodka company (and, by the looks of it, partaking of some generous taste tests as well).

'Ba, you're back,' I said, kissing him on the cheek. 'How did the job go?'

'The shots came out great,' he said. He stepped back from his computer. 'Here, look.'

I leaned over and peered at the screen as he clicked for the slideshow to begin. The vodka was called Satine and was being marketed specifically to target women, a concept that my mother, the only teetotaller in the Badshah family, had found utterly reprehensible. My brother had photographed the model – a full-lipped, creamy skinned beauty – standing in a windswept studio, wisps of hair floating around her sensuous face as she gazed into the distance. She languidly held a pink frosted bottle of Satine in one hand. At her feet cowered a bow-tied waiter, stretching out in his hands a silver tray that held a solitary glass of martini.

'I wanted her to place her foot on the waiter's head, but the client thought that would be taking it too far,' he said.

'No! Really?' I smiled.

Armaan nudged me playfully. There was a reason why he was one of the most sought-after art directors in India. He and his best friend from college, Aroon Malik, owned Double-A Ads, which made commercials and produced print campaigns that were among the edgiest and most irreverent in the industry. They once did a TV spot advertising a hot new bar/restaurant that had a camera panning through the venue, zeroing in on all kinds of implied debauchery. Almost overnight, the place got a reputation for promoting promiscuity, prolific drug use and wanton drunkenness – and was subsequently booked up two months in advance, with lines forming outside almost every night.

'She's beautiful, isn't she?' Armaan said, still gazing at the screen, fingers over lips, staring at the photos in front of him. 'Her name is Ekta.'

'Do you have a crush on her?' I teased. Armaan was exposed to gorgeous girls every day, and as a major player in the advertising game, models would do anything to work with him on one of his campaigns.

'She's different from the other girls,' he said. 'I know you can't see it in these shots, but there's a real innocence to her.'

'So … are you, like, seeing each other?' I asked, a little hesitant. The subject made me uncomfortable. He might be my older brother, but there was a tacit agreement in our household that Armaan wouldn't marry until I did. Of course, given my track record, there arose the question of how long he could wait.

'We hung out a lot during the shoot,' he said. 'Now that the campaign has wrapped up, I think I'll ask her out.'

He switched off his computer and turned his attention back to me.

'How was dinner at Baba's?'

'Weird.'

I knew he was just asking to be polite and didn't really care how dinner went. Of the entire family, he had taken the least interest in the events of the past couple of weeks.

'I'll stop by the office on Monday, see if I can help them with anything. Aroon is going to be around next week, so I can spend some time on anything that Baba needs.'

Baba's staff often called Armaan if they had

issues with their website or needed ideas for a brochure. But he didn't enjoy that work – it wasn't sexy enough for him.

He let out a big, smoky yawn, which I took as my cue to leave.

I strolled down the marble-floored hallway, its silk-padded walls flaunting illuminated paintings by Manjit Bawa and Jogen Chowdhury. The door to my parents' room was shut. I stood outside for a second, about to knock, wanting to have what I hoped would be a revelatory conversation with them. I heard them speaking in low voices inside. I felt like an intruder, so I left.

I went to my room, kicked off my shoes and began to undress. Chanoo knocked and came in, carrying a cup of decaf cappuccino and a plate of biscotti. She set down the tray, picked up the clothes I had flung on my bed, and began hanging them up. I wanted to say something to her, to tell her what had happened at Baba's, what he had said. But I couldn't. Though she had looked after me since the day I was born, she was still the help, and there were rules about these things. It was frustrating. I needed to talk to *somebody*.

After she left, I walked over to a small mahogany desk in the corner, eased into a high-backed pink-and-white chair, picked up my hot drink and gently blew the steam that was still rising off it. I took a sip, let the fragrant warm liquid slide down my throat. I put the cup down again, distractedly fingering its rim.

I wanted to cry, although I didn't know why. There was something about the evening, the dinner at Baba's, that had been filled with discontent. Our previous dinners always had at least some measure of levity. Baba wasn't exactly Mr Charismatic, but he would at least speak a little, ask if we were enjoying the food. That night he had been more sullen than I had ever seen him. Something was changing, and I didn't know what.

I desperately wanted to be exhausted and to clamber into bed. But my body remained glued to the chair, my limbs heavy. I tried to think of all the things I had done that day, all the things that should have cumulatively tired me out. I had woken up early to go to the gym, and later had met an old friend for an iced coffee. A shopping trip with my mother in the afternoon, and then it was home, shower, change, dinner at Baba's. It was a typical day, one filled with pointless activities, but the only kind of day that I knew how to have. I lunched, I shopped, I socialized. I realized now as I thought about it that I was one of the only girls in my clique of monied female friends who didn't do *anything* with their lives.

Quite a few of them were jewellery designers, or fashion designers, writers and restaurateurs. Even my best friend Nitya had a career of sorts: she was a silent partner in a small chain of yoga studios. These girls had leveraged family connections and a boundless supply of capital to anchor their place in the world.

The only thing I had remotely done of any professional consequence, and only since returning to Mumbai, was helping my mother's friends do some small-scale renovations; pity-jobs, I would call them. Aunty Ritu needed new drapes for a bay window in her apartment on Altamount Road. Mona Aunty felt it was time for a bathroom revamp, and could I turn it into something of a spa? I would sit on their Versace couches, notebook in hand, and I could see them thinking, 'Poor thing, still unmarried, we must give her something to do.'

Perhaps because I was the only girl in my family, I had never been expected to contribute in any way. Instead, since I turned twenty, the extended family was simply waiting for me to wed, as if that would take care of everything, become my reason for living. But those fix-ups were few and far in between. I was twenty-six now, stained with an aborted overseas education, and – in the narrow view of so many families –

past my prime. The guys who seemed to be interested in me these days were only so inclined because of who my grandfather was, and those were not the kind of guys I wanted.

Plus, what with everything that happened with Jag so recently, I couldn't even imagine myself going out to dinner with anyone, much less getting married. I had been set back in the worst possible way. Jag, I knew, could never be replaced. I simply couldn't see how I could find with anybody else what I had with him. Though he had asked me to, I just wasn't capable of moving on.

My iPhone buzzed again. A text from Nitya. I looked at the clock – it was past eleven, but Nitya was just getting started. The only time the girl ever saw a sunrise was when she was drawing her curtains to go to bed.

I gave her a call back, and when she answered, I could hear loud music in the background, something by Rihanna. I waited as she made her way to a quiet corner.

'Where are you?' I asked.

'Vishal's party,' she said. 'I thought you were coming. It's rocking.'

I realized that with all the craziness over the past week, I had forgotten Nitya's cousin's birthday bash.

'Sorry,' I said. 'It kind of slipped my mind.'

'What, are you too hot for your friends now?'
she asked, a tart note to her voice. She had been
like that since I'd gone off to London – a little
snarky, not quite the girl I had befriended as a
twelve-year-old in school, when we had shared
glitter pens and giggled in our new uniforms.
Now, Milan described her as a 'classic passive-
aggressive case study'.

'I was at dinner at Baba's,' I replied. 'You know
how hard it is for me to get away sometimes on
Friday.'

'How was it?' she asked. It was suddenly
completely quiet at her end, as if she'd locked
herself in some soundproof chamber.

'Same as always,' I fibbed. 'Usual family chit-
chat. I ate too much mutton curry.'

'Oh Sohana, please,' said Nitya, sounding
exasperated. 'Don't lie.'

'What are you talking about?' Blood rushed
to my cheeks. I recognized the defensive tone in
my voice.

'Baba is mad,' said Nitya. 'Really, really mad.
The whole bloody town knows what's going
on.'

'What's he mad about?' I asked, confused.
'Surely not the newspaper article? That's over and
done with.'

'He's angry with the family,' she said. '*His*

family. *Your* family. He's so mad that he's going to get rid of the company. Every last bit of it. So enjoy being Sohana Badshah for now. Because this time next year, your name won't mean shit.'

SIX

The next morning, I didn't even wait for my parents to wake up. It didn't matter that Saturdays were their sleep-in day. It had taken monumental amounts of self-restraint to stop myself from waking them up right after I had spoken to Nitya. I had been restless most of the night, dissecting Nitya's words, trying to make sense of them. I had been so stunned by what she had said that it hadn't even occurred to me to ask how she knew what she claimed to know.

'Who's it?' my father's sleepy voice shouted out after my third knock on my parents' door. It was just past six.

'Dad, it's me,' I said. 'I really need to talk to you.'

I heard a shuffling inside, bedclothes being pulled off, something falling to the floor as my father fumbled for his glasses on the bedside table. He opened the door, his dressing gown half-wrapped around him.

'What happened, beta?' He stood aside to let me in. My mother sat up in bed, her hair dishevelled, her eyes bleary.

I stood in the doorway, feeling foolish. It wasn't really an emergency. Nobody was dying. There was no fire raging across the house. My parents looked at me with alarm.

'I don't understand what's happening,' I said. 'Nobody's saying anything. I have to hear things from outside. Nitya told me that Baba is really mad at everyone. That he's giving the business away.'

My father looked stricken. He turned around to glance at my mother.

'Give me five minutes,' he said, knotting the sash of his dressing gown around his waist. 'We'll have tea and talk. Okay?'

I waited in the balcony, its glass enclosure cocooning us from the incessant honking that travelled up all the floors and from the grey smog that wrapped itself around the building. It was quieter now, the pace of the city slower due to the early hour. It wouldn't last long. In a couple of hours, the streets would be jammed again, the doorbell ringing with deliveries, vegetable sellers, the servants.

Chanoo came in with tea and toast and the

morning papers, leaving everything on the glass-topped wicker table. I chewed a fingernail, a habit I lapsed into when I was nervous. I wasn't sure if I wanted to hear what my father had to say. Maybe it might have been wiser for me to remain in my blissful bubble, my innocuous world of parties and shopping sprees. I wished Jag were with me. He would know what to do.

My father walked in, hair combed, face freshly washed, my mother behind him. They eased into the couch and poured tea. My father wiggled his toes inside his leather slippers, laid a napkin across his lap. A pair of crows cawed outside, peered at us through beady black eyes.

'I wanted to wait until I could speak to your brothers and you at the same time,' my father said. His face was serious, his voice low. My heart was racing. 'But Armaan has his own schedule, Rajan still unconcerned with these things. So there remains only you among my children who seems to care.'

'Just tell her, for heaven's sake,' my mother interrupted. 'Why are you making such a drama of everything?'

'What?' I asked. 'Stop freaking me out. What's going on?'

My father leaned forward so his elbows rested on his thighs. He tapped his fingertips together.

'Some time back, Baba told us that he wants neither me nor your uncles to inherit the business. He has been, basically, unhappy with how we have done things. Rightly or wrongly.'

'But … but why?' I stammered. 'Is it because of that stuff they mentioned in the article – the problems, the lawsuits?' I was careful not to be too specific. At some point I'd want to ask my father about the fracas with Balu Sachdev. Just not now.

'It is nothing to do with that. We run a big business. Such problems are part of it.'

'But it's a family business,' I said. I was still trying to get a grip on the whole scenario. 'He can't just cut you out.'

'It's his company,' my father said quietly. 'He can do whatever he wants with it. I don't want to get too much into it. But what your friend has heard is true. Baba is planning to sell the whole company off. There had been good offers before. And now, since that newspaper put us on its cover, revealed so many details, there has been talk of a merger. A big German company. We would all cash out, relinquish control.'

I blinked, trying to take it all in. Even though I had barely had anything to do with Badshah Industries, it had been the centre of my family's collective being for as long as I could remember.

It was our touchstone, our claim to a decent social standing, the thing that gave us grace. It funded a secure life. Because of it, I couldn't remember the last time I had to worry about anything. I had never seen the back section of a plane. My closet was full of things that being a Badshah had bought me. When I had wanted to fulfil the desire to be independent, my parents had sent me to interior design school in London. I had stayed in the family home there, and they had deposited money in my account every month. When I had cut my overseas sojourn short, my parents did not judge me. I had fled back home with a broken heart and a story I could not tell them, but they welcomed me back into the fold, assuming that I simply was not made to live alone. They never talked about the monetary investment they had made in an education I would never use because, well, the money hardly mattered.

'Who else knows?' I asked my father.

'We thought it was just us, your uncles and aunts,' he said. 'But clearly, some gossip has leaked out. Amit, Prakash and I objected very forcefully when Baba first told us his plans. It made no sense. We felt we deserved better. But he is a stubborn man. Once he makes up his mind, he will not change it. So that is everything,

Sohana. That is what Nitya was trying to tell you. The future of Badshah is up in the air.'

I allowed the full weight of my father's words to sink in. All this time, I had envisioned Badshah Industries to be jointly and equitably run by my grandfather and his three sons. I had assumed – naïvely, I saw now – that after Baba passed away, my uncles and father would continue running the business in happy harmony. The family members who decided to join the business would be paid well and put on the fast track to the executive floor, eventually taking over from the preceding generation. It would all operate like a well-lubricated machine for decades to come. Nothing could possibly go wrong. But, clearly, something had.

My father said he didn't want to talk about it any more. My tea grew cold. The sounds of the city came jarringly alive below.

'And, really, Sohana, this has nothing to do with you,' my father said, a note of finality in his voice. 'You, anyway, will be married before long, please God, and then you will become somebody else's responsibility. Whatever becomes of the Badshahs, it's none of your concern.'

He stood up. A light breeze came in through an open window and rustled the newspapers.

I looked at my mother, seeking some sort of reassurance, although I didn't know for what. For things to go back to normal? Could they, ever?

She shook her head ever so slightly, as if taking pity on a street urchin.

'Come, Sohana, go back to sleep for a while. Nothing can be done as of now. Later, we'll go to Phoenix Mills, lunch out. Don't worry about these business matters. Let the men handle it.'

I was left alone on the veranda. I walked to the window, stared out at the garish billboards that dotted the landscape, pitching things that everyone wanted and nobody needed. A model dripping gold jewellery, sleek leather furniture framed by calla lilies, a shiny car, the latest cell phone. The skies above Mumbai had always been filled with crap.

In a building across the way, a woman was hanging laundry out to dry. She leaned forward a touch too far and almost fell forward, inches away from tumbling out of the window. My heart jumped. She quickly caught herself, shook off her shock and continued pegging the damp clothes onto the line as if nothing had happened.

The conversation with my parents had left me feeling on edge. I really needed to talk to someone. Milan would still be asleep. Nitya would most likely be nursing a hangover from the tequila shots she must've had the previous night.

Mostly, I wanted to talk to Jag. But we hadn't spoken in a few weeks, and the last conversation hadn't gone well.

At that moment, I just needed to be reassured that we weren't one of those families, the ones that crumbled and fell apart, the ones I read about in society magazines. I wanted us to be normal again.

Below, the traffic started building. It is always rush hour in Mumbai, bullock carts and Ferraris on their way to their destinations. In a little while, my mother and I would join them, navigating our way to a shopping mall, again. I sighed. My parents were right. There was nothing I could do. This wasn't my problem. I was just going to go out and have fun, like I always did.

SEVEN

A plate of chocolate cake sat in front of me, a scoop of mascarpone ice-cream melting into its surface. It was my favourite sweet treat at Café Prato, my favourite restaurant at the Four Seasons which occupied the top of my list of places to hang out in Mumbai.

Nitya appeared in the doorway, glanced around for me, waved and made her way over. Her complexion made its entrance almost before the rest of her did. Nitya's skin was the first thing anyone noticed about her. It was glowing porcelain perfection, as if it inhabited its own orb of light. I was often tempted to grab a magnifying glass and examine it up close, determined to find a single open pore, a strand of facial hair, a pigment out of place.

'How was the massage?' I asked her, spooning the warm chocolate into my mouth.

'Not a massage,' she retorted bitterly, rolling her eyes. 'How many times do I have to tell you?

Shirodhara. Ayurvedic oil poured onto the third eye. I've been doing it every week for the past two months. It makes me very chilled.'

'Yes, I can see that,' I replied, barely concealing the sarcasm in my voice.

Of late, I had come to realize that Nitya could be comatose and still be uptight. For somebody who co-owned a yoga studio, one would've thought she'd be a bit more Zen.

She summoned a waiter and ordered a platter of seasonal fruit and a cup of herbal tea. I stared down at the pool of chocolate in front of me and the steaming pitcher of cream-topped coffee next to it, and felt gluttonous. I needed to drown my sorrows in sugar and caffeine. That morning's conversation with my father had left me more upset than I would admit.

'Here, for you,' I said. 'I've had this at home for weeks.' I brought out from under the table a small gift bag. I had been away during Nitya's recent birthday party and wanted to hand over her present. 'Happy belated.'

She reached over and fished out a small silk purse from the volumes of lilac tissue paper inside the gift bag. She opened it to find the pair of silver-and-seed pearl earrings she had admired during a shopping expedition on the Bandra boutique circuit. I had remembered how much she had liked them, and returned to purchase them the next day.

Now, however, she blanked.

'We saw them at Butter, remember?' I reminded her. 'You tried them on with that black-and-white dress?'

'Oh, right, thank you,' she said, seeming unconvinced. She turned back to the gift bag and continued rummaging through the layers of tissue.

'That's it,' I said. 'Just the earrings.'

She tittered, embarrassed enough for the both of us.

Adjusting her slender frame into her seat, she quickly changed the subject.

'So? What's the latest?' she asked. 'Did you find anything out? You know, about Baba and all?'

So this was why Nitya had called me earlier in the day once she had rolled out of bed at noon. The night before, she had baited me. I had demanded the truth from my parents, and now that I had it, she wanted to sit in front of me with that exasperating 'I told you so' expression she wore so well.

'Yes, he's entertaining offers to sell the business,' I said, trying to be nonchalant, but not feeling the part.

There was that look on her face now, infuriatingly superior.

'Don't tell me your dad and uncles are fine with that,' she said. 'I've heard they're mad as hell.'

I gritted my teeth.

'Tell me, Nitya, how do you know all this? And why do you seem to love it so much?' I was feeling emboldened now, revved up by the carbs and coffee. Nowadays, it seemed as if Nitya and I had begun basing our friendship on meaningless debates and petty spats – skinny jeans versus bootleg, Oberoi versus Taj, Shah Rukh versus Saif. These days, we were at our greatest ease with each other seated side by side at a beauty salon, getting our mani-pedis, flipping through magazines and comparing notes on what we saw in those glossy pages as opposed to having any sort of meaningful dialogue. We used to have a much more sincere friendship. But since my return from London, she seemed a different girl – testy, impatient, shallow. I had asked her a few times if something was wrong, but she had insisted it was all in my head.

Now she seemed stunned by my question, as if I couldn't possibly have the audacity to question her interference in my family's personal affairs.

'The whole town has been talking about it,' she said. 'I was just shocked that you didn't know.' She lifted her hand and gently placed it on her chest, wanting to convey sincerity, compassion. 'I thought it better you be informed. That way, you won't sound like such an idiot when talking to people, gloating about that article about the perfect, happy family.'

There it was again. Nitya's reason for living. Pulling me down when I was up. I didn't want to discuss it any more, at least not with her.

'Forget it,' I said, finally, searching for a way to segue into another subject. 'Are you going to the Moschino event next week?'

Feeling bloated because of my late afternoon snack with Nitya and reeling from my conversation with her, I begged off dinner out with my parents and went to my room. My friend Mayu was having a party at Blue Frog, and while I loved their mojitos and spare ribs, and although I'd told her I was sure to be there, I couldn't face it that night. I didn't need to be in a low-lit place with throbbing music and crowds of people air-kissing and complimenting each other's hairstyles. So I made Chanoo call her, tell her I had eaten something that had disagreed with me. Chanoo glared at me later, convinced that lying on my behalf had cost her valuable karmic points.

The house was quiet. Everyone was out. I was overloaded with calories, lonely, lethargic and desperately lovesick. I was so full of angst that I felt I was living inside a Michael Bolton song.

These were the moments when I missed Jag the most. Whenever I had been sad, or even just tired during those ephemeral days of togetherness, he would wrap his arms around me, press his lips against my hair, tell me everything was going to be okay. I needed him to tell me that right then.

I had been in London only a few weeks when Jag and I met. That I was there on my own had been something of a coup. My grandmother staunchly believed that unmarried girls of a certain pedigree should not go abroad on their own. Ever. Even for an education. Even in 2011. Several years ago, when my little clutch of friends had all flown off to university – some to England, others to America, others still to Switzerland or beyond – my grandmother had dissuaded me from flying the nest, and I, being not particularly ambitious, had not fought too hard. I stayed in Mumbai and went to a nearby college.

But the result of my acquiescence was that

Dadi had remained entrenched in her ways. Now, whenever I needed to be somewhere else – a friend's wedding, some downtime on a Bali beach – Dadi always insisted that someone tag along, a parent preferably, a cousin at least.

So it had come as something of an affront to her archaic sensibilities when my father told her that I wanted to go to London to study interior design.

'She is twenty-six and she wants to go overseas, alone, to learn how to make cushions?' Dadi had said, sardonically. 'Please. Enough of this nonsense. Concentrate on finding her a boy.'

My father was finally able to convince her on three points: that acquiring knowledge in a feminine and non-threatening field would make me more attractive to suitors; that I would stay there in the family home and be regularly visited by relatives; and, most importantly, that all the preeminently well-bred girls in Mumbai were doing it.

Ultimately, Dadi granted me her blessings and handed over her Marks & Spencer shopping list.

My mother flew into Heathrow with me to settle me in to the Badshah abode in Bayswater – a place that could be used by any of the family members during their visits. Mother stayed for a week, helped me shop for groceries (mostly microwaveable), taught me how to use the washing machine, hung up my clothes, tenderly hugged me goodbye, and then, after my first day of the planned nine-month interior design programme, flew back home. Before she left, she handed over a wedding invitation made of red silk which, when opened, disgorged a rainfall of golden paper butterflies onto my carpet. The wedding was in two weeks, of her third cousin's daughter – a close enough relation that a family emissary had to attend, but not so intimate as to warrant postponing my mother's return.

I obediently attended all the parties and ceremonies, returning home at the end of each one to call my mother and report on who attended, who wore what, and the approximate value of the bride's jewellery suite.

The finale of the long, boozy week was the dinner reception in the ballroom of the Dorchester. I had been allotted a spot on a singles' table, the bane of every unmarried person who attends such events. The tables were at the farthest corner of the vast space, covered with powder-blue linen, gold-rimmed plates and glass trumpet vases of ivory roses. I was in a sequined Armani camisole and palazzo pants, with big diamond hoops in my ears. It was bold and modern for a traditional Indian wedding party, but it wasn't as if I was out to impress anyone.

I knew everyone on my table. All the 'boys' were single for very good reasons: there was the twice-divorced polo player, the committed playboy with the growing bald spot and mounting sense of regret, the business whiz who had just done time for fraud. One woman, a forty-six-year old chemical engineer, claimed to detest marriage as much as I could tell she longed for it.

As dessert was being served, my friend Vijay asked me to dance. He was lithe, flamboyant, Eton-educated, and just the sort of man I'd marry if he weren't hopelessly gay. He twirled me around the floor to music that was too loud and we giggled at the portly sixty-year-old man who was chuffing on his cigar, doing the cha-cha to Beyonce and beckoning a hapless waiter for yet another Scotch. The strobe lights beamed brashly, and I was transported, high on music and French bubbly.

My shoulder bumped against something. Hard, definite. It hurt. I turned to face the man who had collided with me.

'Sorry,' he said loudly and kept moving.

I stopped and watched him. At first, I didn't notice the girl he was with, so fixated was I on this wavy haired man in a dark suit, steel grey tie, a silver rod piercing it right beneath the knot. His polished shoes gliding across the floor, his hips gyrating, his wide chest caressed by waves of sound, he moved like he was born to dance. Then the girl moved close to him, pressed her pink-tipped fingernails into his lapel, her highlighted dark brown hair falling to one side of her face. She whispered something in his ear. He laughed, continued dancing. Then the girl turned around, grabbed his hand, led him off the dance floor and towards the bar.

Vijay twirled me again, bringing me back. He had seen me gazing at the man with the steel grey tie. He nodded. 'I know him,' he said into my ear. 'Come.'

I followed Vijay to the bar, around which most of the inhabitants of the singles tables had clustered, hoping to get the last free drink of the night. The girl with the pink-tipped fingernails was talking to someone else, ignoring the man she had just danced with. He was leaning against the edge of the bar, drink in hand, surveying the scene.

'Hey,' he said to Vijay. 'How's it going? Having a good night?' His accent was distinctly American.

'Yes, as good as could be expected at these things,' Vijay replied. He pulled me forward. 'This is my darling friend Sohana. From the fantastically corrupt city of Mumbai. In London to find salvation, apparently.' Vijay turned to me, rubbed my arm affectionately, and then he leaned in and whispered in my ear. 'Go for it. He's hot.'

'Hi,' the man said, extending his hand. 'Jagdish. Everyone calls me Jag.'

'Hi,' I said, taking his hand. It was strong, warm, and covered mine.

'Boy's side, girl's side?' he asked.

'Girl's,' I replied. 'She's my fourth cousin.'

'Makes you practically sisters.' He smiled, stirred his drink, took a sip.

'And you?' I asked.

'Boy's. Well, he's a man, isn't he? Now that he's married? We were roommates at UC Berkeley. We'd lost touch, so I was kind of surprised he invited me.'

'I haven't seen you at the other functions,' I said. As soon as the words tumbled out of my mouth, I realized they sounded vaguely stalker-ish.

'Just flew in yesterday. I couldn't get away from work any earlier. Hung out with all the boys last night, though. That's where I met your buddy Vijay. I RSVPd so late for tonight that I was relegated to a table with the uncles and aunties.'

Another song came on, from Kanye.

'I wonder whose idea it was to play "*Gold Digger*" at a wedding,' Jag said.

'Please,' I said, rolling my eyes. 'Half the women in this room can relate to it. It's their personal anthem.'

'Aren't you cynical?' he said. His tone was teasing.

His eyes drifted towards a bejewelled society matron who was pulling on the mink-trimmed cape that had been dyed to match her emerald-green Tarun Tahiliani sari.

'She looks like she's got a lawn on her back,' said Jag, pointing to her.

'Well, it is cold outside,' I said.

'I know,' said Jag. 'But who gets married in London in late September anyway? They should have waited till next spring.'

'The bride's parents pushed for a quick wedding,' I whispered, resting my glass against my chin. 'She's a bit of a slut, you know.'

He raised an eyebrow, a half-smile lingering on the edge of his lips.

'Are you this nice about everyone or just your relatives?'

I laughed. Suddenly, that night, I felt reckless.

The music had segued into vintage Mariah Carey. The bride and groom slow-danced awkwardly, she tripping on the hem of her lavishly embroidered sari, he stumbling drunkenly into her. I watched them, aware that Jag was watching me. Behind us, the bartender emptied out the oversized brandy snifter that was now packed with pound notes. It looked like it had been a good night for him.

'Where did you fly in from?' I asked Jag, turning back to him.

'I live in San Francisco. It's the place to be for what my field is – environmental sciences, alternative energy systems, natural resource management.'

'Oh.'

'You have no idea what that is, do you?'

'Not a clue.'

'Well then, we'll just have to educate you.' He swallowed the last of his drink and put his glass down. 'How are you getting home?'

He dropped me back in a minicab. His cologne, still fresh after a long night, was woodsy and warm. In the car, we sat closer to one another than we needed to. I toyed self-consciously with my bracelet, ruing the fact that the one good guy to come out of the week-long shindig had showed up on the very last night of it.

'When do you fly back?' I asked, expecting him to tell me he'd be on his way the next day.

'Oh, not immediately,' he replied. 'There'd been some retrenchments at work. We lost a bunch of our funding. I was basically asked to take some time off, a couple of months, at least. Didn't know what I'd do with myself. But when my buddy's wedding invitation showed up, I figured now's a good a time as any to get away. I got a vacation exchange in St. John's Wood. I'm going to be in London for the next eight weeks.'

I was quite pleased, but didn't show it.

Outside the red brick apartment building that was home, he asked for my phone number. He stored it in his phone, tapped in my name.

'Sohana,' he repeated, typing with his thumb. 'What does that mean?'

'Graceful,' I said. It also meant 'beautiful', but I was too embarrassed to tell him that.

'That you are,' he said, giving me a peck on the cheek.

EIGHT

'You know we're like the coolest people here, right?' said Milan. He was jogging briskly next to me down Marine Drive as the sun burnt orange beyond the horizon. Around us were septuagenarians in white cotton kurtas and leather chappals; grey haired men and their slow-footed wives; newlywed women in stiff saris, bright gold chains and fresh henna; kids stopping for a newspaper cone of roasted peanuts. I loved the sea air, the warm breeze, the cratered pavement. I used to come here all the time as a child, sipping fresh coconut water through a bent straw, chasing after my father as he held aloft a brightly coloured balloon. Everyone else was strolling, conversing, communing. But Milan and I zipped through the crowd in our Nikes, looking like we had been teleported there from the New York City marathon.

We stopped, checked our pedometers and pulse rates, and sat down on a ledge close to the water's edge in front of the Air India building.

I was glad he had called that morning. The night before, I had cried myself to sleep, longing for Jag, and for things to go back to normal at home. Prakash Chacha had told Milan the same thing that my father had told me. Just that Milan seemed less bothered than I was.

He took a big gulp of water from a plastic bottle.

'What the hell are you so upset about?' he asked.

'I don't know,' I said. In front of me, a bhelpuri-wala spooned chutney onto a paper tray. 'It doesn't make sense. Baba can't sell the business off to the highest bidder. Our dads are meant to be taking over. It's like Baba is overlooking them.' I shook my head.

'It's not *like* he's overlooking them,' said Milan. 'He *is* overlooking them.'

'That doesn't bother you?' I asked him. 'You don't think it's unfair?'

'What I think doesn't matter,' said Milan. 'I'm just a nobody in the family. Like you.'

I was offended at that. I may not exactly have been contributor number one, but I was *not* a nobody.

'Listen,' said Milan now, with a little more sensitivity. 'Maybe not everything will change.

Depending on who ends up buying Badshah, our dads might continue to work there, if they want to. Otherwise, they'll each get a big chunk of money and can go do anything they want. Don't you think your father has ever wanted to be someone other than a Badshah employee?'

'Actually no, I don't,' I replied. 'The family business is all he's ever known. I don't know what he'll do with himself. This is their legacy. The business is meant to go from Baba to his sons to the grandsons. That's how it works in a joint family.'

'We're a bloody *dis*jointed family,' Milan said, resting his elbows on his knees. 'The truth is, if our dads could disown each other, they would. There's no love lost between them.'

I bit my lower lip. I hated what he was saying – even though I knew it was true. Lately, I had been noticing it more and more. Friction whenever the brothers got together, as if they would rather be somewhere else, anywhere. At Baba's house a few weeks earlier, I had heard shouting from behind a closed door, curse words being used between Amit Uncle and Prakash Chacha. They both emerged red-faced, picked up their drinks, went back to their wives, and didn't say a word to each other for the rest of the evening.

'I'm not saying there's going to be no drama,'

Milan said. 'But we are an Indian business family. Drama is our middle name.'

I leaned over to tie a loose shoelace. I wondered why all those astrologers and numerologists who were so frequently consulted by my family had not seen this coming. Or, if they had, how come they never said anything. Gurdas, the bald, rotund spiritual advisor who was Baba's go-to guy for everything from the location of a new property to the naming of a new bride, had foreseen only good things for the family – unity and harmony. I had heard him say as much himself.

I reminded Milan of this.

'Please,' he replied, stretching his hamstrings. 'Gurdas is a moron.'

I laughed. Gurdas had been the man who had advised that all the Badshah grandchildren have names that ended with the letter 'n'. Most of his ilk usually suggested the first letter for the child's name, picking an initial that was most congruent with a family's birth chart. But Gurdas had focused on the last consonant, something that Milan would refer to forever after as 'ass-backwards'. Given that I was supposed to have been another boy in a family overflowing with them, my parents had pre-named me Sohan. It was only after they recovered from the shock of having had a baby girl that they stuck an 'a' at the end, effectively changing my name, and, according to Gurdas, my destiny. I was the only girl. And, out of the seven Badshah offspring, I was the only one whose name ended with a different consonant.

'So my dad, and your dad, and Amit Uncle – they just get put out to pasture, like old cows. Is that what you're saying?'

'That's *exactly* what I'm saying,' said Milan, standing up now to resume his sprint. 'And you, my dear cousin, will become the ultimate heiress. You act like there's something wrong with that.' He turned his back to me and started running again. I raced to catch up with him.

NINE

One morning the following week, as my father ate runny eggs on toast for breakfast, I told him I wanted to go to the office with him. He almost dropped his fork.

My mother looked up from her bowl of khichdi.

'I only ever go to the office on Diwali. I'd just like to see it on an average day,' I said. My interest had been piqued by the newspaper report. Business was never discussed at home or at family gatherings – another one of Baba's many rules. 'Plus, with things changing …' My voice drifted off, but I could tell that my parents knew what I wanted to say. If Baba did what he had been threatening to and sold the business, I may never be allowed back into the offices again. And that realization filled me with sadness.

And there was something else: as futile as the quest may have seemed, I still wanted to get to the bottom of the Badshah–Sachdev case. I hoped, perhaps naïvely, that a cursory visit to the offices might shed some light.

Dad glanced sideways at my mother. She shook her head, went back to her food.

'I guess there's no harm,' she said, addressing my father. 'She'll get bored in half an hour. I'll send the driver back for her.'

Based on what I'd seen in Hindi films, I expected every employee on the top floor of the Badshah Industries building to stand up and bow deferentially as I walked in. I was, after all, a rarely sighted offspring of one of the bosses, a gossamer apparition. Me being there on that day should be a treat, something for them to talk about in the lunch room afterwards. They would marvel at my poise and graceful demeanour, my warm but regal style. My sudden appearance at their place of work would make their day.

But there, on the decidedly ordinary looking 'executive penthouse' floor of the business that my grandfather had built, the employees barely looked up. My father strolled a few paces ahead of me, nodding a perfunctory good morning to the support staff who sat in neat cubicles down the main thoroughfare of the office. Some glanced in my direction, a couple of the women smiled, looked me up and down, and nonchalantly looked away.

'My daughter, Sohana,' my father said, introducing me to his PA, Raghu, a lanky, bespectacled fellow in a short-sleeved shirt and purple tie. Raghu looked puzzled at my presence.

'She expressed an interest in visiting today,' my father said wearily, answering the unasked question.

'Good morning, ma'am,' said Raghu. 'Can I call for some tea, coffee for you?'

'Nothing, thank you,' I said, smiling sweetly, eager to impress.

I followed my father into his spacious cabin whose large windows overlooked Nariman Point. His desk was clear, organized – so much so, it looked like it served almost no purpose. A computer buzzed to life at the press of a switch and the Badshah Industries logo appeared as his desktop picture. A minute later, a white-capped housekeeping staff came in with Dad's tea.

'So, what is it you'd like to see?' he asked. I had barely been there five minutes and he already looked impatient, as if he had something much more pressing to be getting on with.

'Well, what do you do here?' I asked.

He glanced up from his computer, a thin frown on his forehead. A barely audible ping indicated that his emails had finished downloading.

'What do you mean what do I do?' he replied. 'I work. I help run the business.'

'Yes, but, like, what?' I persisted. I felt like a child at career day. I also felt slightly ashamed. I was twenty-six years old, not entirely stupid, but I had very little idea what really went on within those walls. In fact, I was ashamed to realize, I had chosen to remain in the happy state of blissful ignorance until I'd felt it was all about to be taken away from me.

My father breathed heavily and glanced at his watch. He sat down in his chair, its tufted leather squeaking to accommodate him.

'I'm mostly responsible for the hospitality unit,' he said. From a drawer, he pulled out a stack of glossy brochures and fanned them out on his desk. 'We own hotels in a number of countries. These are the latest.' He fished from the bottom of a pile a media kit about the Enchantee Group in Europe. 'We've just acquired this company, which owns boutique hotels in France, England, Mauritius and Ireland. The article mentioned it.'

I rifled through the folder, which had pictures of each individual property, room rates and nearby sightseeing destinations.

'Of course, I'm not involved in the day-to-day running of any of them,' he said, loosening his tie. 'But the overall picture, looking at annual projections, profit and loss sheets, where cutbacks can be made and profits maximized ... those are my responsibilities.'

'And the uncles?'

'Amit is the property expert. Can look at a place, anywhere in the world – an apartment complex, an office building, it doesn't matter – and he can say right off whether we should buy it or not. Does all the numbers in his head, makes an offer on the spot. Without the need of any Vastu Shastra. He just *knows*.'

For a moment, my father's face softened, as if talking about his brother had awakened an affection he rarely felt any more.

'And Prakash primarily looks after the steel mills, although he has his fingers in a lot of pies. When he was young, Baba would take him sometimes, show him the iron ore being smelted, the molten iron being poured. You know, Baba, when he was a teenager, worked in a steel plant? Properly? With his hands?' My father lifted up his own hands now, and stared at them.

'Dad, can I ask you something?' I said. It was time to bring up the business with Kismet Corporation. It was in print now, for everyone to see, and I wanted to find out what had happened.

'What is it?'

'In the *Journal* story, there was something about a lawsuit that had been settled. What was all that about?'

My father took a deep breath and scratched the side of his head as he was wont to do whenever he wanted to think about what he would say next.

'It is a small business matter between our family and someone in America. It has been dealt with. It is nothing for anyone to be concerned about.'

'Anyone?' I wanted to shout out. 'I'm not *anyone*.' I was his daughter, a member of the family, and I wanted to know. But, as I realized while looking at my father, in his eyes my interest was sudden, fickle and too late. He didn't want to be drawn in any more.

'Dad, aren't you going to miss being here?' I asked. 'If Baba sells?'

'These things take a long time to happen, Sohana,' he said gently. 'The right buyer, good negotiations, consultations with lawyers and finance people. It doesn't happen overnight. And depending on how any deal is structured, some of the executives may be able to stay on. But I can't think about that now, beta. We still have a business to run.'

Raghu came in, said there were calls on hold and someone waiting for a meeting. Dad switched back into business mode, and pulled out folders and files. It was time for him to get back to work.

Raghu offered to walk me out, and led me down more glass-enclosed offices and cubicles, their walls covered with framed college degrees, their desks holding tiny plant pots and statues of Ganesha. All those lives, contained in tiny white open-faced boxes. The people there were strangers, essentially, yet they knew more about what went on in my family's business than I did.

'Hey, Soh, what are you doing here?' I heard someone behind me. It was my cousin Karan, fresh from his trip to Dubai. He was clutching a slender brown briefcase and his bright eyes told me he was happy to be in the office.

'Hi,' I said. 'Just came for a visit.'

He raised his eyebrows.

'Okay,' he said. 'Jo bhi. Have fun, yaar. Gotta run. Million goddamn things to do.' He went into his cabin and shut the door.

Sharan was an office over, with only a wall separating him from his younger brother. He wasn't around, but his assistant was. I remembered her from Diwali since on that day, being a Catholic, she was the only one not dressed in fancy new clothes. Today, she was in a tight black skirt and a sleeveless yellow top with a ruffle around her ample bosom.

'Hi,' I said, extending my hand. I glanced at the name on her desk. Mary Verghese. 'Mary, right?' I said, pretending to be smarter than I was.

She looked at me like she knew better. She stood up, grabbed my hand. Her short bob framed long-lashed eyes and she had a slight, upturned nose. Her lipstick glowed pink beneath the fluorescent light.

'Very nice to see you again, ma'am,' she said. 'Mr Sharan is out at the moment. Can I give him a message?'

'Just tell him I said "hi",' I replied.

I walked on. There were empty offices, sparsely furnished, with city views, but nobody to enjoy them.

'What are these?' I asked Raghu, who was still standing next to me, patiently. 'Why is nobody here?'

'Some layoffs last year,' he said, a little sadly. 'Badshah Sahib was restructuring.'

'Oh,' I said. 'Seems a shame.'

Raghu looked at the empty spaces and nodded.

'Mr Badshah had hoped, some time ago, that there would be more of you in the company.

Many grandchildren, but only two here.' I could swear I heard him tut-tutting under his breath.

'Thanks for showing me around,' I said, wanting to make him leave, wanting to be alone. 'I can see myself out.'

I hopped into the elevator and decided to stop at a couple of random floors. There were eleven storeys, but we occupied only six. The lower five had been leased out to other businesses. At today's rentals for commercial space, that income alone would be a small fortune, enough to sustain many families for many years.

A sign in the hallway of the eighth floor announced it was for shipping at one end, accounts on the other. Further down was human resources, finance (how was that different from accounts, I wondered), order fulfilment, processing. Each level was abuzz with activity, but quiet, controlled. Everyone seemed focused. I wandered around, noted that most people seemed to know who I was and smiled cordially, and one or two even asked if I needed anything. But my presence seemed to cause little diversion and even less interest. I was just another visitor on just another day, and they gazed at me vacantly. The boss's only granddaughter I might be, but I had no standing there, and they knew that.

At the main entrance, I spotted my driver

beyond the glass doors, waiting. The security guard stood up as I walked past him, raised his hand to his head in a half-salute.

'Goodbye, ma'am,' he said, wobbling his head, looking straight in front of him. The driver got out of the car, held open the back door, and I got in, as clueless as I was when I had entered.

TEN

My mother had arranged lunch with the chachis and Jaanvi, a usually lacklustre event that took place every month or so outside of the various other commitments the Badshah women usually had: the volunteer work, the religious ceremonies, the shopping expeditions. These supposedly girl-bonding sessions were usually initiated by my mother, who felt a great need to hold the family together, even if it was not necessarily falling apart – not visibly, anyway.

'This is what joint families do,' she had said to me once, when I had complained about having to tag along. 'A family that plays together, stays together.'

Now, we were all attempting to 'play together' at Tote on the Turf, which, like so many people who frequented it, was famous for being famous. It was half-full, its cavernous space and high ceilings making it look emptier than it was. By the time my mother and I arrived, Malini was already there, with Jaanvi by her side. A few minutes later, Preeti strolled in, stopping to chat with a table of socialites.

Malini stood up and kissed me and my mother on both cheeks. Her make-up was even more pronounced than usual – dark pink blush that looked like it had been stencilled in, silvery blue eye shadow, her dyed brown hair teased and backcombed and sprayed so ferociously that it barely moved. Because of her harsh make-up, Milan, in his more uncharitable moments, would refer to her as 'the drag queen'. Today, in her semi-translucent chiffon wave-print blouse and multiple strands of pearls woven with gold, she looked like the ultimate cougar. Her lips were as puffy as a Moroccan ottoman, her brow lines all but wiped away thanks to her good friend Botox. At fifty-five, given her long legs, full breasts and feline features, she could have been stunning, sensual. But with all the transformations she had sought to undergo – some of them not up to the mark – she had been reduced to a caricature of herself, a Beverly Hills cliché transplanted to the heart of Mumbai.

In comparison, Jaanvi looked almost homely. The odd strand of grey stood out from her otherwise frizzy black hair. She was wearing a loose orange top over jeans, like an ascetic.

Though she was seated, her handbag was on her lap, its strap loosely wound around her shoulder, as if she might have to make a run for it at any moment. I felt a stab of tenderness for her.

'Hello, ladies,' Preeti said, reaching us and pulling out a chair next to mine. 'Are we slumming it again? Truth be told, I was in the mood for some pani puri from Kailash.' She winked at me.

I loved Preeti. She was outspoken and had a nimble mind. An Ivy League-educated woman from an upper middle-class professional family in Boston, she had caught the eye of my uncle Prakash on a New York subway. He was there on business; she was down for the weekend from Cornell, where she was majoring in psychology. He had noticed her on the E train when he got on at 53rd Street. He said later that he was taken in by her intelligent green eyes, leading him to believe she was Afghani. He was getting off at the same stop and as she walked down the platform, a small folding hairbrush fell out of the outside pocket of her bag. My uncle ran to pick it up and called out after her. She took it from him and thanked him. They rode the escalator up to the street together, an opportunity he took to ask her where she was from and about the genesis of those green eyes.

'I'm Indian,' she had said. 'Well, I'm from here. But my parents were born in Bombay. We used to go back every summer.'

He told her that was where he lived. She knew the street he grew up on, the school he had gone to. She took the card he proffered and said she might call. She did.

When Prakash Chacha flew back home ten days later, he already knew he would marry her. Baba had initially been reluctant, having had no role to play in the alliance. He wasn't familiar with Preeti's family. But as soon as he got to know her, he gave in. She was one of the most genuine people he had ever met. The family welcomed her without a dowry.

'So,' said Malini, wrapping her red-tipped fingers across the stem of a champagne flute. She had only recently acquired the habit of drinking champagne in the middle of the day. 'I hear our lovely Sohana here made a little visit to our office the other day. How *lovely!*' she said.

I wondered if her vocabulary extended beyond the use of 'little' and 'lovely'.

'Yes, Chachi. I've never gone when it wasn't Diwali. I just wanted to drop in.'

'And did you run into my two little busy boys, running that whole place?' she asked, blinking her spiky eyelashes at me.

'Actually, only Karan,' I said. 'Sharan was off somewhere.' As if she didn't know. Within seconds of my leaving the building, details of my visit would have been transmitted and circulated on the virtual Badshah Bulletin Board.

'Hmm,' she said, taking a sip. 'And what little lessons did you learn there?' Her tone was mocking, snarky. She seemed riled by the fact that I had dropped by the office at all.

My mother picked up on the tension and immediately sought to get rid of it.

'It was nothing, Bhabhi,' she said. 'The girl was just curious. Come, let's order.'

Malini turned to her menu and we considered the conversation dropped.

'And how are you, Jaanvi?' Preeti asked. 'Keeping busy?'

My cousin-in-law nodded. I hadn't seen her in a couple of weeks and her face looked bloated. Could she be pregnant? I was almost about to ask her when I realized what a colossal faux pas that would be. I stuck a breadstick into my mouth instead.

'Yes, very busy with my charity work,' she replied. 'Two big fundraisers coming up.' She said something about wells in rural areas and schools for children.

At least Jaanvi was trying to carve out some sort of life for herself. It saddened me that she and I weren't closer. She was, in effect, my sister-in-law, another young woman in a family drowning in testosterone. We could have been each other's allies and confidantes. But there had never been any closeness, nor any attempt to create it on either of our parts.

I had always been struck by the ludicrousness of her marriage to my cousin. While Sharan was driven and robust, Jaanvi was bland and insipid. Sharan had been Mumbai's most eligible bachelor, his appeal unfurling across international lines. Girls flew in from Delhi, Singapore and London to see him. Mothers of prospective brides shoved each other out of the way at parties to propel their daughters forward into Sharan's reproachful gaze. He, for his part, milked it for all it was worth. He ran around with starlets and models, and had a litany of flight attendants on speed dial. His lifestyle had landed him in the gossip rags, contravening Baba's edict about our family maintaining as low a profile as possible. So when he was referred to for the third time on Page Three as 'the playboy princeling', Baba shut the whole gig down. He rounded up the troops – in this case, his nearest and dearest with daughters of a certain age – and got the word out. He would pick a girl for Sharan from among them.

Jaanvi Sippy was twenty-three, an introvert, not the kind of girl to make trouble, the offspring of a prominent Lagos shipping family. She came with a hefty dowry and enough Swiss bank accounts to prop up a faltering monarchy. As Baba had said to Dadi after he had got off the phone with Jaanvi's father, he had decided that 'she will do.'

As lunch was being served, Preeti was talking about her professor father who was about to retire. Her younger sister had just had her third child. Her brother had been laid off from his New York finance job. She wanted to send money, but he wouldn't hear of it. She crunched on her salad and talked about the everyday experiences of her relatives; I found something endearingly refreshing in what she was saying. I felt my body relax, sinking into the mundane details of other peoples' lives.

Throughout, I noticed Malini looking my way, smiling her tight smile, jaw clenched. She seemed weird that day, secretive.

The bill came and she drew out her credit card. There was the usual faux clamouring over who got to pay.

'Does it really matter, girls?' Preeti said, snatching it out of Malini's hand. 'It comes out of the same bank account, no matter who picks up the tab.' She laughed. 'Let's all say "thank you" to Baba Badshah.'

The waiter took the credit card. Jaanvi was playing with some crumbs on the table.

'I need to ask you all something,' I said. It was not like me to be this direct. I usually took a backseat at these lunches. My mother turned to face me, a slightly stricken look in her eyes. Malini was suspicious, Jaanvi indifferent. Only Preeti seemed to be curious about what I wanted to say.

'How much do you all – the Badshah women – know about the business?'

Jaanvi stopped forking the crumbs and looked up at me.

Malini swigged the last of her champagne. 'Darling, what kind of an idiotic question is that?' she said. 'We know as much as we need to.' She flicked her long fingers in the air. She was tipsy, and trying to be light-hearted and naughty. But it wasn't working. She struck me as a little pathetic.

'Sohana honey, why are you asking?' Preeti said, looking at me with those translucent eyes. I was glad she hadn't wasted her psychology degree. She volunteered two days a week at a women's shelter, helping victims of abuse. I could see how anyone would trust her.

'That newspaper article just got me thinking,' I

said. 'I know so little about the family business, and I suddenly feel quite ashamed. And now, with everything changing ... Baba perhaps selling ... I wish I'd done more. Known more.'

'Well, I'll tell you what happens in my house,' Preeti said. 'Prakash comes home, tells me what kind of a day he had, who he had lunch with, anything important that took place. I host dinner parties for the people he does business with, so, of course, I am privy to certain aspects of the business. When something big happens – a new acquisition or a major problem – he always shares it with me. It is a vast, complicated business, with many arms, but I do think it's important for the wives to keep on top of things.'

She noticed the hesitant, regretful look on my face, and put her hand on mine and smiled.

'It's never too late,' she said.

The waiter finally returned, and it was time to leave. On the way out, my mother, Jaanvi and Preeti visited the rest room. I was left standing with Malini, waiting for our drivers to bring the cars around. She was about to visit her friend in the hospital and needed to stop and buy some flowers. My driver was the first to reach the entrance. As I turned to kiss my aunt goodbye, she grabbed my arm, pulled me close and placed her lips near my ear.

'Sohana, beti.' I felt the tips of her nails piercing through my sleeve. 'There are things happening behind the scenes that your little brain can't understand. Stop interfering. Okay?'

I knew that look in her eyes. I remembered it from when I was a little girl – from a slumber party with my cousins at Malini's house. I had started crying for my mother. But Malini wouldn't let me go home. She forced me to go to sleep. When I refused, she made me stand in a corner. All the boys were in another room, too young and sleepy to care. It was three in the morning. Finally, my eyes were heavy, sore from the tears. I begged her to let me go to bed. She slapped me and left me standing in the corner until I collapsed with exhaustion on the rug. One of the servants found me the next morning, a rivulet of drool on my chin, a paisley pattern imprinted on my cheek.

I never forgot that night. And somewhere in my subconscious, I knew I would never forgive my aunt for it.

Now, her hand still rigid around my arm, I was stunned, speechless. I didn't know what to say. My mouth hung open. The other women appeared. Malini let go of me, kissed me coolly on the cheek. My mother ushered me into the car and we set off for home.

ELEVEN

Priyadarshini Park was one of the few places in the city where my mother allowed me to walk alone. It could be seen from our home, and she knew that I was familiar with every inch of the place. She couldn't deny me the opportunity to have solitary time there. It was her refuge when she needed to get away, and allowed it to be mine too. For me, it had everything: the ocean at one end, an expanse of green in the centre, a row of tall buildings circling its perimeter. In its midst, I felt secure.

I went there occasionally to get away, although I didn't really know from what. Boredom, perhaps, the restless ennui of my life, as if traversing across patches of ill-watered grass would somehow provide answers to questions I hadn't even asked myself yet. That day, still reeling from Malini's bizarre and mystifying comment, I really did need some alone time.

I sat down on the grass, which itched through

my track pants, and then pulled my knees up to my chest and watched the world walk by. I shut my eyes for a second, thought of Jag. It must be early in the morning in San Francisco. He would be awake by now, probably out for his morning run, up and down the hilly streets of the city, before heading to work. I wondered if he thought about me, the way I did about him. I wondered if he thought of me at all. He had called me a week after I had returned to Mumbai. I had been ecstatic to hear from him and waited for him to apologize, to tell me he had made a mistake, and he was catching the next flight over to set things right. But he didn't say any of those things. He had called to ask how I was. To say he was sorry for the way things turned out. He hoped I was doing okay. I cried on the phone, my cool evaporating. I asked him if there was any way we could start over, told him that I missed him desperately. He said to me, with a heart-breaking finality, 'Let it go.'

It had been less than two months since he walked out the door of my family's London home, and time, despite what people had said, had not eased the pain. My heart was still broken. I still longed for him. The end had come so suddenly, so abruptly, that it had taken me three days to stop crying, four to have a proper meal, six before I could pack my bags and flee home. After things had ended, I couldn't even bear to be in the same city in which I had known him. Nitya had told me I was being weak, childish, that I should toughen up, that he's just a guy after all. But she was wrong. He was *the* guy. He was the one for me – until he wasn't.

The day after my fourth cousin's wedding, true to his word, Jag had called. It was a beautiful day of sunshine in September, the kind of blue-skied afternoon that makes the weather during the rest of the year tolerable. Was I in the mood for an early evening bite?

We met outside the Covent Garden Tube station. He was already there when I arrived, his suit given up in favour of a pair of rugged denims and a long-sleeved black T-shirt. He was as handsome as I remembered – so it hadn't been the cocktails playing tricks on my mind the night before. He was leafing through a guidebook, looked up when I tapped him on the shoulder, and leaned in to hug me hello. He suggested the Crusting Pipe, a place with live classical music in the courtyard. He led the way, as if he'd lived in the city forever. We ordered grilled chicken – free-range, he wanted to make sure – herbed risotto, arugula salad, a carafe of chilled chardonnay. The musicians started up, the swell of the strings stirring my insides.

'Rachmaninoff,' he said. 'I played violin as a kid. I gave it up years ago. I wish I hadn't.'

I gazed at his fingers, long and supple and strong.

'Shall we start?' he asked.

'What?'

'Educating you. About renewable systems, peak oil, all that good stuff?'

'If you must.'

He grinned. 'Nah. You don't need to learn about solar-powered infrastructure tonight. Let's just hang. Cool?'

'Cool.'

The wine was crisp, the food delicious, and we could hear each other over Liszt.

His parents lived in upstate New York; his dad was a property developer and he had an older sister. He had toyed with the idea of joining the family business. But, he said, helping the world through energy conservation proved too much of a draw.

'My folks have absolutely no idea what I do for a living,' he laughed. 'They say they do, but I know they don't. When I told them it was a non-profit venture, they figured I'd be sleeping on friends' couches for the rest of my life. They're happy that I am able to pay the bills, though. I guess the last thing they need is their thirty-four-year-old son going home and living in their basement. Tell me about you,' he said, refilling my glass. 'What are you doing in London alone?'

'I just needed to get away,' I said, the wine relaxing me. 'Being, like, one of the only singles among lots of couples, I felt like I didn't fit in any more.' I paused for a second, regretting my words. All the find-a-husband books warned against even using the word 'married' on a first date, insisting it was a turn-off. Me telling him I left Mumbai because I was single also told him that I wanted to be married, and, apparently, no single guy wanted to hear that.

He broke off a piece of bread, dipped it in a shallow dish of olive oil and swirled it around so his fingers were soaked.

'You're lucky that you can just leave like that. That you have the support.'

'I'm studying interior design,' I said. 'It was something to do, something my family could understand. We have relatives here, and a place for me to stay. My parents were okay with it.'

'What do they do?' he asked. 'Your family?'

'Steel,' I said. 'A few other things, but steel, primarily.'

A flash of realization came to his eyes, as if that one word – steel – was all I needed to say for him to know who I was. Steel meant money.

'What other things?' he asked.

'You know, to be honest, I'm not completely sure. They own quite a few properties in India, that much I know. My grandfather is very low-key. It's a privately held company and he pretty much controls everything. He doesn't talk business outside of the office. And I'm not there, so I don't know a lot about what goes on. I'm sorry.'

'Please, don't apologize,' said Jag. 'It's none of my concern, anyway. I was just curious. It's still brave, what you've done. It takes guts to leave the life you know and to try something new.'

Everything about this man was open and inviting. Twenty-four hours ago, I didn't even know him. But over a casual dinner at a Covent Garden restaurant, he seemed to see who I was, and we didn't need to say anything more about it.

He paid the bill. We walked through the glass-ceilinged market that was packed with shoppers and diners. I was trailing behind him, cushioned by strangers. He turned around, grabbed my hand and led me through the crowds until we emerged on the other side.

My hand stayed in his all the way through the Tube ride home, and while he walked me to my building. We stood outside. One end of my scarf fell loose. He picked it up, twirled it around my neck and patted it into place.

'There,' he said, his voice soft. I could smell the wine on his breath. He leaned forward, kissed me on the cheek, a whisper away from my lips. He rested his face against mine for a fraction of a second and then pulled away.

'I had a great time tonight,' he said.

'Me too,' I replied. I didn't want him to go.

'I'll call you,' he said.

He turned, skipped down the stairs outside the building that led to the street. I stood and watched him, a yearning in my heart. I went upstairs to an empty apartment, an empty bed, and felt lonelier than ever.

He did call. The next day. And the day after. We saw each other again, and again. While my heart was being swept up in this magical, sudden romance, my head was telling me to be cautious. I was not one to believe in perfect relationships, having had it drummed into me by my mother that the romance and grandeur of a wedding had absolutely nothing to do with the rigours and realities of marriage. I had seen Sharan and Jaanvi struggle through their own.

But what was happening with Jag was as close to perfect as could be desired. It might have had something to do with the fact that he had nothing else to do but be with me. There was no work to commute to, no last-minute meetings and rushed deadlines. A relationship free of outside stresses can be, as I discovered, quite a sublime thing. He was in London to explore, to let the days unfold and take on a momentum of their own. The fact that I had entered his world was a bonus, he kept telling me. The icing on the cake. My surprise appearance at the start of his eight-week sabbatical had turned it from a self-enforced vacation to an impromptu honeymoon that signalled, as much for me as for him, the start of a new life. By the end of week three, we were committed. Even though he lived in San Francisco and I in Mumbai, neither of us was going anywhere.

'I've sealed off my exits,' he said one night over a couple of glasses of Baileys. We were in a small pub near my home. He was rubbing my hands between his. Orange flames ensconced in a brick-framed fireplace at the far end were warming the room.

'Huh?' I said.

'I'm in this. I'm not going anywhere.'

He was wearing a pale blue sweater, butter-soft

to the touch. I tugged at a loose strand of yarn at his wrist.

'These past three weeks have been incredible. I came to London because I needed to get away and think, to make some decisions about work. And then I met you out of nowhere. Both of us have homes to go back to. But we can figure that out.'

I was staring at him. Three weeks of our romance had translated into four dinners, two lunches and five movie dates. Still, he had yet to kiss me. It was bizarre. Back home, we would have been engaged by now.

'I wanted to take it slow,' he said. He was still talking. For a man, he talked a lot. 'I haven't really let myself fall for anybody, not after Nikki.'

Nikki. The ex-wife. He had told me about her midway through week two. They had met while he was attending a conference in Sonoma. He knew soon after the wedding that he had made a mistake. They divorced after a year.

I would have thought I would be perturbed that the man I was so rapidly falling in love with had been married to someone else before, had already given himself in a way that men, supposedly, think long and hard before they do. But, I was surprised to realize, it didn't bother me in the least. Malini, crass as she was, would often describe such marriages as 'foreign expeditions' – short-lived, exciting for a time, but rarely lasting.

'Well, boo-hoo for Nikki,' I said. 'You're mine now.'

While dropping me home, he came upstairs, took off his jacket, kicked off his shoes and got comfortable in an armchair. I put on a Regina Belle CD. I had stumbled upon Preeti's collection of 1980s R&B: Luther Vandross, Teddy Prendergrass, Anita Baker. She had left a stack of her sultry music CDs behind in the family's communal music collection. I was sure Jag would call it 'whiny chick music', like Milan did.

'This is great. Relaxing,' he said, and closed his eyes.

'Yes,' I agreed. The last thing I wanted to talk about was music. The last thing I wanted to do was *talk*.

I sat on the carpet, near his feet. A pot of rosehip tea lay steeping on the coffee table. I edged closer to his legs.

His head rested on the back of the armchair, his eyes closed. He didn't move.

He opened one eye, gazed down at me.

'Are you trying to seduce me?' he said, a cheeky smile playing on his lips.

My skin burned hot in embarrassment. I inched away.

'Soh, listen,' he said suddenly. 'I've been here three weeks and I haven't been to Trafalgar Square yet. Do you maybe want to do that tomorrow? Go feed the birds?'

I sighed. An hour earlier, this man had professed his love for me. Now here we were, alone. It was raining outside. There was sexy music playing in the background. And all he could think about was *pigeons*?

'Sure,' I said. 'Maybe after school? We're doing a lesson tomorrow on crown mouldings.'

He put his hand on my head and began to stroke my hair.

I closed my eyes, waited for him to ease down on the carpet next to me, to finally make his move.

'Right, tomorrow it is,' he said, leaping up. 'I'll call you in the morning.'

He gave me a hurried kiss on the cheek and was gone in a flash, shutting the door behind him.

I caught sight of his brown leather jacket draped across a chair just where he'd left it. I grabbed it and opened the door. He was still in the hallway, waiting for the elevator.

'You left this,' I said, and dangled it on my finger.

He looked at me thoughtfully. The doors to the elevator opened. For a split second, I thought he was going to get in, that he would tell me he'd get the jacket from me the next day. But he stepped away, and back towards me.

He took the jacket from my hand. He was standing in front of me now, neither of us saying a word. I was barely breathing.

I'm not sure who moved first. But in the space of a second, his lips were on mine. We were back in my apartment, the door banged shut. He had me pressed against a wall. I couldn't breathe. I didn't care.

I had forgotten to draw the drapes. The pale morning sunlight woke me. My head was resting on his chest. He was still sound asleep, breathing heavily, a bare leg stretched out from under a crumpled sheet. I covered it, pulled the blanket up over both of us and curled in closer to him, if that was possible. My movements woke him.

'Hey,' he said, slowly opening his eyes.

'Hi. Slept well?'

'Like a log. You?'

'Hmm.' I snuggled, wrapped my arms around his waist.

He rubbed his eyes awake, turned, propped himself up on one elbow.

'Last night was fun,' he said, smiling naughtily.

I could feel my cheeks warming. Jag had not been my first. But, I knew after the night that had passed, I wanted him to be my last.

'Can I ask you something?' I said.

'Given that we're naked in your bed, I think you can pretty much ask me anything.'

'What took you so long?'

'What?'

'We've been dating for three weeks. You were dragging your feet. I felt it the first night I met you, that I wanted to be with you. I was beginning to think you weren't interested.'

He sat up, swept his hand through his sexily dishevelled hair. 'You know, three weeks isn't a long time before falling into bed,' he said. 'I'm kind of an old-fashioned guy.'

I was ashamed now; what kind of a girl must he think me to be!

He rubbed his finger on my cheek.

'I'm kidding,' he said. 'The truth is, I felt it too, at the wedding reception. It's just that you're not the sort of girl a guy should be messing around with. I wanted to be sure.'

'Are you now?'

He got back under the covers.

'I'm sure I want to be with you, yeah.' He leaned forward, kissed me on the nose and gathered me up in his arms again.

I never did learn about crown mouldings that day. And Trafalgar Square was put off for another afternoon.

Jag's vacation exchange in St. John's Wood was left mostly unattended after that night, with both of us having agreed that it made sense for him to move most of his stuff to my house.

We were almost never apart. If I could skip classes, I did. When I returned home every afternoon, Jag would be waiting for me. He was an inspired cook, surprising me with pumpkin ravioli or almond-crusted salmon. We took walks in Hyde Park, soaked in sudsy baths, sometimes talked till two in the morning. I found myself telling him things I thought I had forgotten long ago, dredging up dusty memories spliced with hurt: how I'd so often been ignored by my boy cousins because I was a girl, or the romantic relationships that had turned sour when they had been so full of promise. He was the sort of man who didn't even flinch about his new girlfriend's old heartbreaks. Instead he listened, absorbing every word.

Over those weeks, he revealed himself to be the kindest person I'd ever known. When I was fasting and we had stopped at a little café so he could have a bite to eat, he excused himself and went to the Tesco next door, returning with a pile of fruit which he asked the restaurant to cut up and serve to me. When I came down with the flu, he soothed my aching body with hot towels, back rubs and copious cups of tea fortified with freshly grated ginger.

I knew this lovingly crafted attention was largely because it was the first flush of a new romance. But there was something enduringly solid about Jag, something that told me he could always draw from a limitless pool of goodness, that his generosity would never run out. I felt that my life was safe in his hands. After having dated monied Mumbaiites who cared more about the colour of their car interiors than about my feelings, who had ended things with me when they feared that a call with a marriage proposal from Baba to their families was imminent, Jag's earnestness was irresistible, and impossibly sexy. He made me want to be better – more capable, well-rounded. He told me to challenge myself.

'Here,' he said one evening as I came back from school. He held up strings of floury white tagliatelle. 'I made this. Turns out your marble counter top is perfect for rolling out dough.'

'You made pasta from scratch?' I asked him, perplexed. 'Who does that?'

He laid it down on the counter, gently, as if

he were holding vintage brocade that would fall apart at the slightest rustle.

'I'm going to salt the water and put it on the heat,' he said. 'When it boils, just place the pasta in, stir it occasionally, keep an eye on it, okay? I'm going to jump in the shower.'

I did as he asked. But instead of watching the pot until the water boiled, I got on the phone, put away my books, folded the laundry ... until I heard the smoke alarm go off in the kitchen.

Jag was already there.

'How do you burn water?' he asked me, holding up the charred pot. 'Isn't it just my luck to be in love with the only Indian woman in the world who can't cook?'

All I had heard in the conversation was 'in love'.

After that, he tried a few more times to engage me in his love of cooking, showing me how to make a reduction, a hollandaise, a roux. But as he stood behind me by the stove, stirring a saucepan with a smooth wooden spoon, I would turn around, kiss him and turn off the flame. After a while, he gave up.

'Just promise me,' he had said, letting my lips move across his face. 'That one day, you'll learn how to take care of yourself.'

'I promise.' I kissed his closed eyelids and tugged off his apron.

'So I've been thinking,' he said.

It was the end of week six. In fourteen days, his sabbatical would be over. He had got a call from his boss. There was still a job for him, if he wanted it, with a pay cut, which he'd agreed to. He loved his work and wanted to go back to it. So far, we hadn't discussed what that meant for us. I just assumed it would be taken care of, like Jag always took care of everything. It would fall into place.

'I hate it when you think,' I said. 'It means you're going to say something smart that will make me feel stupid.' It was true: out of the blue, Jag would launch into a dialogue about Reaganomics, agricultural subsidies, the military-industrial complex, things I had neither knowledge about nor interest in. But I would nod respectfully, mumble 'that's terrible', and wait until the commercial break got over so we could get back to our TV show. I loved his worldly intelligence, but did not delude myself about having even a smidgen of it.

He reached over and grabbed the remote. We were in our pyjamas, watching *The X Factor*, our hands shovelling deep into a bowl of freshly made popcorn. He turned the TV off.

'We need to talk,' he said, serious.

Crap. I pulled my hand out of the bowl, rubbed the butter and Parmesan onto a napkin. I knew that voice, that look. I had seen it in other men before Jag had come along. He was ending things with me. My heart sped up.

'Relax,' he said. He put the bowl onto the coffee table, angled his body towards me, held my still-greasy hand. 'I've been trying to figure out what's next for us. But before I do, I need to hear from you. Where do you see things going?'

It was such a typical Jag question. He was all about talking things through. I wanted him to be a bit more of a chauvinist, to take charge of things. I didn't want him to *ask* me where things were going. I wanted him to *tell* me.

'Please, Jag, don't put this on me,' I said. 'Don't take all the romance out of it. You decide.'

'Feminists of the world rejoice,' he said. 'You're a credit to women's libbers everywhere … Okay, here's the thing.' He softened his voice, the mischief gone from his eyes. 'Me getting on a plane in two weeks doesn't mean this is over. In fact, I'd like to think it's just the beginning. Would I be wrong in presuming you're thinking the same?'

'You would not be wrong. No,' I said.

I looked at him now through the prism of my family. On paper, he had all the best credentials: right surname, age, family background. He would be thoroughly vetted by everyone, most scrupulously by Baba. But in the end, my family would see his innate goodness. They could only love him. For now, he had been my secret; apart from Milan and Nitya, nobody knew about Jag. As much as I loved him, I couldn't tell my parents. They didn't need another disappointment. I couldn't tell them until I was sure, and I couldn't be sure until Jag was.

'You'd like San Francisco,' he said. 'It's a really beautiful city. There's a big Indian community up in Fremont.' He was trying to entice me with my own heritage.

'That's not important to me,' I said. 'I'm sure I'd like your city. But only because you're in it.'

'I told my mother a little about you,' he said. 'She's thrilled. A girl from India, no less. Never thought she'd see the day. Dad's travelling, but when he's back next week, she'll tell him. They can't wait to meet you.'

I was delighted – Jag, the divorced man cautious in love, telling his parents about a girl he'd met meant that I was more than a girl he'd met. I was *the* girl.

'So, what next?' I asked.

He moved in closer to me, rested his forehead on mine. Then he pulled away and didn't say anything. Instead, he reached behind him and produced a small velvet pouch. From it, he took out a chain with a sapphire peace emblem. He strung it around my neck, centred it.

'Goes great with my frog-print pyjamas,' I said, tears gathering in my eyes.

'Wear it always,' he said.

After Jag had gone to bed, I called Nitya.

'He said he loved me,' I told her, euphoric. 'That he's going to find a way for us to be together. Then he gave me a chain with a pendant. It was *so* romantic!'

'Talk is cheap,' she said. 'If he really wanted to be with you, he'd be on the phone with your dad by now. Real love doesn't wait, Soh. He'd be flying to Mumbai tomorrow.'

'Oh, so you're the expert, are you?'

It was a low blow. Shortly before I had left for London, Nitya had had a major relationship fiasco. Juno Malhotra, Mumbai's chief cad and the town's reigning boozing billionaire, had flown her to Vegas on his private jet, checked into The Mansion at the MGM Grand, and gone out while she acquainted herself with the six-bedroom suite and private butler. Juno had planned dinner at

Joel Robuchon. She was convinced he was going to propose over Cristal champagne and Osetra caviar. She had her Marchesa dress laid out on the bed and had booked a Mother of Pearl body treatment in the spa. She was going to be ready for the night of her life.

But the night never happened. Instead, Juno had gone on a fantastically debauched bender, physically assaulting a security guard at the Wynn and scooting from the scene in someone else's Maserati. He was finally arrested for, among other things, driving under the influence of alcohol. The police also found a tiny packet of cocaine in the glove compartment, which did nothing to help his cause. The Indian ambassador had to be called, as well as Juno's uncle, a high-ranking minister. Juno languished in a jail cell while Nitya was asked to check out of the room by noon and find her way back to Mumbai.

So perhaps I could allow her a little cynicism.

'Take it from me,' Nitya said. 'If he wants to make things work with you, he won't wait a minute longer. Everything else is just an excuse.'

At that, I hung up, fingering the pendant on my neck but unable to rid myself of the nagging feeling that maybe Nitya was right.

Five days before Jag was scheduled to fly back to San Francisco, I helped him move the rest of his belongings from the vacation rental and pack the bags for his journey home. With every garment I folded and every pair of socks I bundled into a neat ball, I could feel a rising anxiety. I hated that I was soon to come home to an empty apartment whose every feature would be rendered charmless by the absence of the man I was now hopelessly and irrevocably in love with.

It was nearing Christmas and I was supposed to fly to Madrid to visit some relatives. But the thought of not having Jag around when I returned was more than I could bear. I just couldn't imagine life in London without him.

To add to the mounting sense of desolation, he was yet to make any firm plans for us to see each other again. Maybe Nitya had a point. Maybe it was all talk; he would get on that plane and forget all about me. Maybe I was a fling, after all.

Four days before his flight out, we finally made it to Trafalgar Square. After, he wanted to go shopping for gifts. He bought Union Jack alarm clocks and tin cans of tea for colleagues. For his mother, we went to the food hall at Harrods where he stocked up on overpriced chocolates wrapped in beribboned boxes, and then bought bottles of tarragon-infused vinegar for his sister, a whiz in the kitchen like him.

'I feel sick you're leaving,' I said as we rode the Tube back home, laden down with packages. 'I'm going to miss you terribly.'

'Me too.'

He leaned across to kiss me. I waited for him to say something more, to indicate when we might see each other again. He looked down at the bags between his feet.

'Well, at least we got the shopping over with,' he said.

The next morning, I began repacking his bags to accommodate his new purchases.

'There's stuff I can't jam in here.' I pointed to a pile of clothes on the floor. On the top lay the pale blue sweater that, for some reason, reminded me the most of him.

'Oh,' he said, then thought for a moment. 'Can I just leave them here with you?'

'What would the point of that be?'

'I'll collect them when I'm here next, dummy. I'm planning to come back for a weekend next month. Already made my bookings.'

I turned my attention back to the overstuffed suitcases, jubilance written on my face.

The day before his flight, I had to stay at school later than usual to finish a project. As if 'Basic Building Codes and Systems' was not deathly boring in itself, having to write an 800-word essay on it while the man I loved was waiting for me to spend our last night together before we were to be separated for weeks on end was, to me, an injustice beyond compare, a massive violation of human rights.

When I got home, Jag's suitcases were packed and locked, upright in the foyer. He was sitting on the couch, his head in his hands, one foot tapping restlessly.

'Hey,' I said, taking off my coat. 'What's going on?'

He glanced up at me, his face more serious than I had ever seen it.

'We have a problem,' he said.

'What happened?' I asked, trying not to sound panicky.

He paused, as if trying to find a way to say what he needed to.

'My dad just got back to Jersey. I talked with him, told him about you, who you were …' He fell quiet. His face was pale. 'Your family screwed my dad over. There's a lawsuit. I knew that my dad was dealing with some legal stuff, but I never knew the names of the people involved.'

'I don't know anything either.' I sat next to him, put my hand over his.

'My dad freaked out. He says I can't be with you.'

I lifted my hand.

'I … I don't understand,' I said. 'I don't have anything to do with the business.'

He rubbed his forehead.

'I've never heard my dad so angry. Look, I think I should go. I still have use of the other apartment till tomorrow. Let's just take some time, okay?'

'What time?' I wanted to yell. In twenty-four hours, he would be on a plane. Surely he couldn't leave, not like that.

'You sealed off your exits,' I said quietly. 'You said you weren't going anywhere. The first night we spent together, that's what you told me. '

'I meant it. Everything was going great. I loved you. I *love* you.'

'Then don't leave,' I said, desperation cleaving through my voice. 'We'll work it out.'

He stood up. Tears tumbled down my cheeks which were still cold from the air outside. I held on to his fingers, tugged at them.

'Please,' I begged. 'Please don't go. I'll leave them behind. My family. If I have to choose between them and you, I'll choose you.'

The words rang hollow in my ears. I knew they were untrue, even as I was saying them.

'I'm not going to ask you to do that,' he said. 'And it wouldn't make a difference anyway. It's not you. I just can't be with you right now. Not with all this mess.'

He pulled out his phone and called a minicab. Though the driver was fifteen minutes away, he went down, dragging his bags with him. The door slammed shut. Behind it was the plastic bag stuffed with the clothes he wanted me to keep there for him, the pale blue sweater right on top. He had forgotten it.

I remained motionless on the couch, staring at the marks his suitcases had left on the carpet.

'That's friggin' nuts,' said Milan.

It had taken me three days to collect myself to even speak on the phone. In the hours after Jag left, I kept waiting for him to walk back in, tell me he'd made a horrible mistake, beg me for forgiveness. He didn't.

'Do you know anything?' I asked.

'Not a thing,' Milan replied.

His voice made me long for home.

'I just don't get it,' I said, crying again. 'He told me he loved me.'

'Soh, listen to yourself. This kind of crap happens all the time. Affairs are made and broken based on family relationships. Why are you so surprised? Do you think your dad would have done any differently if the situation was reversed? It's family marrying family. Period. Always has been.'

I was sobbing again now.

'Look,' said Milan. I could tell from his voice that he needed to go, that there was probably some girl he was rushing to meet. 'Forget about him. Go to Spain. Have fun, get wasted, meet some other guys. Live it up.'

I shredded the moist white Kleenex I had been holding in the palm of a clenched hand.

'I don't think so, Milan,' I said. 'I'm coming home.'

TWELVE

It was another Friday night at Baba's. I watched as Milan and Pawan battled it out over chess and mused on how different they were, how disconnected.

Milan was muscular, sexy, and had taken over the mantle of Mumbai's Most Eligible Bachelor from Sharan. Quick-witted, brilliant, he glided through parties like a young presidential contender and wore vintage rock tees, designer jeans, custom-made shoes, the works. Nothing stuck to him: traffic violations, miffed exes, business associates who felt wronged – Milan made everything right with a dazzling smile, a fist bump, a charming word or a soothing rub on the shoulder. Nobody could ever stay mad at him for long.

Pawan on the other hand was thin, bespectacled, often sullen. He had tried to emulate his twin's innate cool, thinking that Ed Hardy T-shirts would do the trick, until Milan let him know that such a wardrobe was inherently 'douchey', compelling Pawan to revert to his collared checked shirts and high-waisted pants. He had graduated from MIT in Aeronautics and Astronautics.

Milan had ended up on the opposite end of the country, opting for Pepperdine in Malibu. He bought an almost-new Porsche and every update on his Facebook page was a picture of him with yet another blonde at yet another beach. Later, when his father asked him what he had learned, Milan simply shrugged and said, 'Stuff.' But his small portfolio of successful self-started businesses and an enviable knack at day trading proved that his half-hearted education had not let him down.

Both boys had arrived home from college within days of each other, Pawan wiser and more serious for the experience, Milan tanned, sporting a single stud earring and with a plan to make an appointment with the family doctor to check for possible STDs.

And now, Pawan was hunched forward, frowning and pondering his next move. His long-sleeved shirt was buttoned at the wrists. Milan was sitting back in his chair, arms folded over an artfully faded Rolling Stones T-shirt, legs stretched out and looking heavenwards, as if not interested in the dance of the rooks and knights in front of him. I could tell by the fierce intensity on Pawan's face that he wanted to win.

As kids, Milan usually let his twin brother beat him in sprints down the street or in late-night games of carom, spurred on by pity for his more awkward, less socially capable brother. By the time they were in their teens, Pawan had figured out that he and his brother weren't always on a level playing field, and since then went out of his way to trump Milan wherever he could.

Now, Pawan moved his queen just so that Milan could take it. Milan didn't realize what kind of trap he'd fallen into. Suddenly, his twin moved his rook.

'Hah! Checkmate!' he shouted victoriously, toppling Milan's king. Milan shrugged, got up and poured himself a drink.

Dinner was on the patio, and dining al fresco was a refreshing change from eating in the stuffy, wood-panelled dining room. Even in the dusky light, the laburnum tree that stood at the near end of the garden adjoining the patio shone with its rich yellow foliage. Next to it, the pink cassia was also in full bloom, its green leaves dotted with strawberry pink buds. Dadi loved her garden and spent many hours there, and her attention to it was evident: terracotta pots boasted curry leaves and tulsi plants, and delicate coriander and potent cardamom. Everything prepared in her kitchen contained something planted by my grandmother or plucked by her hands.

I walked over to Milan, crunching a cheese straw dipped in spicy ketchup. He was deep in conversation with Armaan, who seemed to have stunned the rest of the family by walking in, so infrequent were his appearances. He had come straight from the office, saying the only reason he was able to leave early was because Aroon had stepped in to finish a project they were working on for a new luxury resort in Goa.

Armaan and Milan stopped talking as I approached; conversations in my family always seemed to grind to a halt when I showed up.

'Hey, Sis,' Armaan said, taking another gulp of his gin and tonic. 'What's the gossip on the other side of the lawn?' He looked over at the rest of the family milling about. 'Malini looks especially terrifying tonight,' he said. 'What the hell happened to her mouth? All you can see is lips galore.'

'She had a new treatment. To make her lips look fuller,' I said. 'They inject fat from the buttocks into them.'

'No wonder she talks so much shit,' retorted Milan, and he and Armaan chortled loudly. For two supposedly intelligent and sophisticated men, they were more juvenile than my baby brother.

A bell sounded, summoning us to the table.

'Like friggin' cattle,' Milan said, putting down his drink and spitting out a lemon seed that had ended up in his mouth. 'They're rounding up the flock.'

Armaan checked his watch. 'That's fine by me,' he shrugged. 'I've got a hot date.'

'Ekta?' I asked. 'So that's all happening, is it?'

'It is super happening,' he said, grinning. 'I'm taking her to Shiro.'

I felt a pang of envy. I loved it there – the sound of the waterfall, the bulbous red glass lamps cascading from the ceiling, the curtained beds upstairs where you could recline in a velvet kimono with a platter of sashimi.

Dinner was over in twenty minutes, with Baba standing up to indicate its end. But he sat down again. The table went quiet, with only the faint pinging of my younger brother's DS emanating from the farthest corner of the table. He'd clearly snuck it in somehow. Baba noticed it now. I figured that the next time we met for dinner at his place, there'd be a metal detector by the front door. Rajan, alerted by the sudden silence, quickly turned off his gadget.

'Everyone, we will have tea in the hall,' said Baba. 'I want to talk to you as a group.'

Milan and I looked at each other. This had never happened before. Typically, once we finished dinner, we all made our way home. Moving to another room to have a discussion was unheard of. It was almost civilized, like something out of *Downton Abbey*.

There was no lapse in time between leaving the patio and heading to the living room. No trips to the restroom, no stepping out to make a phone call. Everyone grabbed a seat, Pawan and Rajan reclining on big embroidered cushions on the floor, Malini sitting primly on an armchair, her legs crossed daintily, like a Kate Middleton wannabe.

Baba came in, Dadi by his side. Behind him was one of the servants, carrying his chair from the dining room. He resembled a Rajput maharajah, missing only a tame tiger at his feet. He had always had a remarkable ability to quiet a room simply by showing up in it. He could have walked into a classroom full of unruly six-year-olds, and had them working studiously at their desks in no time. Dadi stood next to him, like an underling. I stood up to proffer my seat to my grandma, but she held her hand up, telling me to stay where I was.

Baba brought his fingertips together and gazed around the gathering. He was still strong and broad at eighty, as magnificent and intimidating a man as he'd ever been. He used to bounce me on his knee as a child, introducing me to everyone as his 'little Lakshmi'. He would tell everyone that I had brought him wealth, that it was only after I was born that his fortunes changed. I'm not sure I ever really believed him, ever thought it was more than just his particular brand of spin. But I did so love being cuddled when he placed me on his lap, and nuzzling my face in his neck and kissing him on his coarse, stubbly cheek. I don't know when the ease and comfort I'd felt around my grandfather devolved into fear.

'There has been a lot of talk, inside this family and outside it,' he said, drawing out every word. 'It is time for me to speak to you honestly. To place all the facts before you.'

Everyone stiffened. Though there was no anger in Baba's voice, though he seemed composed, our nerves were tense. I could feel feet twitching all around me.

'Some of you younger ones have been spoken to by your fathers. They have told you of a decision I have made. A very difficult one. Do all of you know what I am referring to?'

Heads nodded slowly: Sharan and Karan,

Armaan and I, Milan and Pawan. Only Rajan didn't respond, looking as bored as he was befuddled.

'So then, as you know, after much prayer and deliberation, I have decided not to pass on the company to one of your fathers. My sons will have enough money for the rest of their lives but they will not inherit Badshah Industries.'

I turned to look at my father. His head was lowered. I stood up from my place on the couch next to Milan and walked over to where Dad sat with my mother. I took my seat next to him. Baba stopped speaking as I moved, waiting for me to settle down again. All eyes were on me as I exhibited my impromptu act of alliance. Malini looked at me with suspicion, as if I was dressed in Arab garb at a US airport.

'So now that neither Amit nor Jeetu nor Prakash will be taking over, I have to take some other decisions. I have had very good offers to sell, especially since that article came out. But …'

But. A word that either gave hope, or took it away.

'But I've decided that you all deserve better than to see the family business go to an outsider. You need a legacy. So the company will be passed on to one of the grandchildren. One of you.'

He paused. There wasn't even the sound of any of us breathing.

'Of course, that being the case, to whom the company will ultimately go has been very clear.' His eyes scanned the room again, settling on Sharan.

Malini was the first to speak.

'Baba, you have made the right decision,' she said, uncrossing and crossing her legs. The lacy hem of her slip was peeking through her dress. 'It is time for you to relax, let one of the young ones take over. You just look after yourself in your old age.'

'Kiss-ass,' Preeti whispered behind me, a wicked grin on her face. I loved how she always said what I was thinking.

'I don't need your approval,' Baba said sternly to Malini, making her smug smile disappear. He turned back to Sharan.

'Come here, beta,' he said.

Sharan stood up, walked over to his grandfather, looking as if he were about to be knighted.

'Sharan, you are a hard worker. You have made me proud.'

Sharan blushed. It was clear this was the first time he had been praised by Baba.

'You are the firstborn of my firstborn. By rights, everything should go to you. But …'

There it was again. Another but. Another fault in the plan, a detour in the road.

'The others should be given a chance too. They should be allowed to prove themselves.'

Sharan looked as if every drop of blood had been suctioned out of his face. I looked around the room. Milan suddenly had a steely look in his eyes that I'd never seen before. Pawan played with a tuft of carpet, yanking the threads distractedly. Malini's eyes widened as she struggled to regain her composure.

'So, my children,' Baba said, holding on to the arms of his de facto throne to stand up, 'do your best. Bring something bold to Badshah. Revolutionize it. Be smart. Take risks. You all have a chance. Whoever does the best, has the most interesting ideas for the business and proves his worth, will be named the new CEO. If I am not happy with what you do, I will revert to my original plan to sell. I will be watching. And most importantly,' he said, lowering his voice, 'no mistakes.'

Dadi stepped back to let Baba pass. Her lips parted fleetingly, as if she were preparing to say something. But she didn't. She pulled the pallav of her sari close around her and stiffened her back.

I should have stood up and spoken out. If that story in the newspaper had helped expedite Baba's vague plans, then certain questions about its contents needed to be answered. If the boys were going to fight for the company, they needed to know what exactly they were fighting for. Transparency. The truth. How hard could that be? My head was spinning. I almost opened my mouth to ask the question that still gnawed away at me: What was happening between the Badshah family and Balu Sachdev? And why had *my* life been ruined because of it? But now, in the light of the topic of discussion, it seemed like an inconsequential matter.

Instead, it was my big brother who finally spoke.

'*Any* of us, Baba?' Armaan asked. 'Even those who don't have much to do with the business now?'

'Any of you,' he said. 'Sharan, Karan, Armaan, Milan, Pawan. Rajan is a child, still.'

Outside Baba's house, everyone lingered, not getting into their cars right away.

'That was weird, right, Didi?' Rajan said. He was holding my hand. I was thirteen when he was born and used to care for him like he was my own.

'Yes, very,' I said. 'But I don't want you to worry, okay?'

'Shit,' said Milan, sauntering up to us. 'Heavy stuff. Hey, Bro, what do you think?' he said, nudging Pawan, who shrugged and walked off.

'What are you going to do?' I asked.

'What do you think? I'm going to win the bloody company. Whatever Sharan can do, I can do better. I got my Pepperdine degree, remember?' he said, winking. 'I didn't just sleep around for four years.' He paused. 'Three, maybe.'

My father tapped me on the shoulder. The car had come and it was time to go. Armaan came towards it.

'What happened to your date?' I asked him.

'She's still on a shoot,' he said. 'We fixed it for tomorrow instead. It's just as well. I think I want to hang with you and the folks tonight.'

Milan whispered in my ear before I got into the car after my family.

'Listen, I don't think Armaan is interested. So, you'll help me, right? Be my partner in crime? I'm your number one cousin, remember?'

'Of course, Milan,' I said. 'Anything for you.'

THIRTEEN

My favourite times with my family came at the end of long evenings, after some social event, when everyone was tired but still had enough energy for tea and gossip. We would all be in our nightclothes, and gather in the quiet of our living room with a pot of freshly made chai and a late-night snack on the table. My father would put something by Anup Jalota on the CD player, and I would sit on the couch cross-legged, holding a cup, delighted and grateful to be with my parents, to see them at their least fussy, their most relaxed.

On my way home from Baba's that evening, I knew we would have one of those chats. After Friday night dinners, with Nitya usually pestering me to go to some club, I'd often arrange to meet up with friends. But that night, I didn't respond to any texts or calls. Nothing could lure me. I just wanted to be home. And the fact that Armaan would be there too – a rare occurrence of late – made me doubly enthusiastic.

We sat now, all of us in robes and slippers, my make-up removed, hair knotted into a ponytail. Even Rajan, who should have been in bed by then, sat with us, drinking cold chocolate milk and nibbling from a packet of shortbread. We were no more the family occasionally seen in the pages of society rags, glammed up and shiny, but our real selves – ordinary, quiet and a little troubled.

Armaan was in a pale yellow cotton kurta instead of his typically all-black attire. He was stretched out on the billowy brocade couch, his elastic legs propped up on the marble-topped coffee table. As spacious as the house was, it couldn't seem to accommodate him. It didn't even seem to suit him. He belonged somewhere leaner, sparer, more modern, not in this feminine rococo fiefdom. I had made changes to the interiors after I had returned from London, a task assigned by my father, a touching act of encouragement after my botched stab at an education. Our house now was luxe, glossy, a little overdone in parts, but I had designed it without thinking of Armaan's sensibilities, as if he weren't even part of the household.

'At least things are now clear,' Dad said. 'At least

it's an open race. I have not agreed with much that
Baba has done, but I agree with this. Everyone
should get the opportunity.'

A large gilt-edged wall clock ticked in the
background. It was close to midnight. My mother
yawned. Armaan looked like he was desperate for
a cigarette, but he never smoked in the house.

'How do you feel, Dad?' I asked.

'I'm fine,' he said, waving off my concern.

Rajan stopped chewing and turned to look
at us.

'No,' I persevered. 'Really. How do you feel
about Baba cutting you out? It must hurt.'

Before London, I would never have asked him
that. Before London, before Jag, I took everything
at face value. But my time with Jag had taught me
that things are rarely as they seem, that everyone
has their triggers, their vulnerabilities. That deep
inside, grown men are little boys, needing their
daddies to be there for them.

I saw that in my father now, and was
unexpectedly moved by it. I reached out, put my
hand on his. He drew it away quickly.

'Beta, I am fine,' he said, a hard edge to his
voice. 'I cannot do anything about the decisions
your grandfather takes.'

He turned to Armaan, away from me.

'You asked a question at Baba's house, whether

all of you had a shot. Are you thinking along those lines?'

Dad was all business now. He was in the war room.

'I'm just thinking,' drawled my brother in his typically laconic way, 'that Sharan shouldn't just make off with the goods. Okay, he's been the one who's spent the most time there. But business is a changing game, Dad. And the players can change any time.'

Dad smirked a little, a familiar glint returning to his eyes.

'Shabaash. You are a good boy, Armaan. Smart, capable. Your advertising business is all well and good. But how rich can you really become? How powerful? Running a company like ours, the world is in your hands. Take it. Try.'

'I don't know, Dad,' Armaan responded. 'I have a business partner. We're booked with campaigns till the end of the year. And we are close to being able to buy another floor in the building so we can expand. Things are going well. I can't just leave like that. I was thinking more about Milan and Pawan. I didn't want them to feel like they don't have a chance. But I don't think I'm the guy.'

I agreed: I couldn't see Armaan, a born renegade, running Badshah Industries ... But when had I been able to see anything?

My father looked disappointed.

'What about me, Dad?' Rajan asked innocently. 'Can it wait till, like, I finish school?'

My father reached out, ruffled his youngest child's hair. 'You don't worry about anything,' he said, smiling.

'Ma, did you see the expression on Malini's Chachi's face when she realized her beloved Sharan was not going to just be presented the top job on a platter?' I said now. 'It was brilliant!'

Barely three months in London and the word 'brilliant' had stuck with me. I used it all the time.

'Enough of this talk,' Mom said. 'It's late. Time to sleep.' She paused for a moment, looked at Armaan and Dad. 'But,' she said, a sparkle in her eye, 'there will be interesting times ahead.'

All of us were sealed off in our rooms, but I was still unable to sleep. I went to my closet and brought out one of the large poster boards I had transported home from London, on which I had done plans of fictional homes I would never decorate. I touched the swatches of pale gold satin chenille, the picture of the geometric-patterned day bed, the room anchored by a ruby red Murano chandelier. The week I had finished that pretend-client presentation had been a month after I had met Jag, the days when I was falling hard for him. I had thought of him as I had sketched a sunken marble tub in a bathroom and drawn details of silken curtain cords. The elation I had felt with him in my life had exalted every creative sense in me.

Now, I flipped the board around sullenly, as if doing so would dislodge Jag's lingering presence. The back was blank. I grabbed a black pen and wrote out the name of every cousin and, next to it, drew two columns. In the empty spaces, I wrote why, in my estimation, that cousin should be named the new chief of Badshah. In the second column, I wrote why he shouldn't. When I was finished, I chewed on the tip of the pen, considered what I had written, tucked the board away behind a suitcase in my closet and went to bed.

FOURTEEN

I didn't recognize the caller ID on my phone, but I answered it anyway.

'Miss Sohana Badshah?' I heard an efficient, high-pitched voice.

'Yes?' I said, tentatively.

'My name is Manjuli Khosla.' She paused, as if waiting for her name to register. 'I am with the *Daily Business Journal*.'

'Yes, I know who you are,' I said coolly. I was puzzled. Why was this woman – whom I considered to be responsible for the recent turbulence in my family – calling me?

'I hope I'm not disturbing you, miss, but I wonder if I could ask you a couple of questions.'

'What is it you want?' I was at the tailor's, being fitted for the blouse of a sari, my arms aloft like a scarecrow, my phone nestled uncomfortably in the crook of my neck.

'I also write for the weekly magazine attached to the *Journal*,' she said.

I knew of it. *Sunday* was, I have to admit, one of my guilty reads. There was a sensationalist vibe to it, a fun, gossipy sensibility. The journalists and editors who worked there refused to fawn over the town's rich, famous and celebrated.

'There is a rumour going around town that your grandfather does not wish any of his sons to inherit the company, that he may sell it or pass it on to one of the grandchildren,' she said. 'Specifically, Sharan Badshah. We have been trying to follow this lead for some days. I have called a number of people at Badshah Industries for a comment.'

I said nothing.

'I was hoping that perhaps, as someone not directly involved in the business, you may be able to shed some light on the reports.'

'Why would I talk to you?' I said sharply. 'I wish you people would leave us alone.' I was about to hang up.

'Whether we get a quote from the Badshah family or not, the magazine is going to run something,' she said. 'The reports from within the business community are enough for another feature. And the response to the piece in the *Journal* was so overwhelming that my editor has demanded a follow-up. I wanted to offer you the opportunity to set some things straight. Off the record, if you prefer.'

I had to think quickly. The original story had done enough damage; I hated imagining what trouble a follow-up would cause. I wanted to have nothing to do with it.

But then I remembered the black box at the bottom of the feature, the snippet of information about Kismet Corporation and Balu Sachdev. If anybody had more information on that, it would be Manjuli Khosla.

'Miss Badshah, are you still there?' she was saying.

'Fine, I'll talk to you off the record,' I said. 'But you'll have to do something for me too.'

I was taken aback when she joined me at my regular table at Frangipani the next morning. I had always envisioned female business journalists as being sharply put together, all no-nonsense chignons and designer briefcases and French manicures. I imagined them to be like the girls at *Vogue*, looking like the high-powered people they wrote about.

But with Manjuli, there was neither chignon nor designer briefcase nor French manicure. Her hair was tied in a loose ponytail held together by a cotton handkerchief. One side of her small body was weighed down by a heavy satchel, its leather strap fraying. Her nails were bitten to the core.

Frangipani was a popular venue, and meeting in such a public place was perhaps not a wise choice. My family and I were regulars there at the Sunday champagne brunch, where most of my friends would show up in chiffon frocks and stilettos, inevitably carrying a new Hermès Birkin. Even now, a Wednesday, the sunlight-filled restaurant in the basement of the Oberoi Hotel would soon be crowded with society mavens stopping for a bite during a day packed with shopping expeditions, fittings and hops to the gym. But it was early yet, and while the place was busy, it was now populated mostly by American business executives and European tourists. From what I could ascertain, there was nobody I knew.

'Thank you for agreeing to meet me,' she said. 'Nobody at your grandfather's office would even return my calls.'

'I think we all feel that the story was so intrusive, nobody wants to invite any more trouble.'

'I was just doing my job, miss,' she said. She ordered a mango lassi for herself. 'My editor wanted me to write a story on your family. Even though you are a privately held concern, and not answerable to shareholders, there has always been quite a fascination about the Badshahs. It was unclear what the extent of your grandfather's business empire was. But with a little digging, our team uncovered a lot. It was the element of surprise. A relatively prosperous family, living quietly … It has shocked everyone to know how much the Badshahs really have, how much you are worth.'

'I don't believe even half of it,' I said. 'We're not one of those people. We don't live like that.'

'Maybe,' she said. 'But facts don't lie. And, miss, we have all the facts. There has been no demand for a retraction. Why? Because everything we wrote was true.'

She paused and pulled out a tattered red notebook from her bag. I looked slightly askance at it. I thought journalism would be a bit more high-tech than that these days, with digital tape recorders and MP3 players.

It was as if she read my mind. She smiled. 'I find a pen and paper to be most reliable,' she said, then turned to a clean page and clicked her pen.

'Miss Badshah, can you confirm or deny that your grandfather, Darshan Badshah, has chosen to bypass his three sons when handing over the empire, and that it will either go to one of the grandsons or the entire business will be sold off to a third party?'

I said nothing.

'Please, Miss Badshah, don't worry. It will never be traced back to you. I will quote you simply as "a source close to the family".'

'I can't say anything,' I said. I was nervous. I regretted having agreed to meet her. What was I thinking?

'Confirm or deny?' she repeated.

I could do neither. Denying it would be a lie, and confirming would make my father and his brothers look like incompetents in the eyes of their friends. It was mostly my father I worried about. He would have to deal with the shame of it soon enough – why would I put him through that now, force him to relive the humiliation in the pages of a national magazine?

But I also knew I had to give her something. If I wanted to get from her what I went to get, I needed to part with information that would be of some value to her.

'Look, Miss Khosla, let me make you a deal,' I said.

She leaned forward.

'There are changes afoot at Badshah Industries. What they are I am not at liberty to say right now. But …' I raised my eyebrows and paused for effect. 'If you allow me a little time, I will return the favour by giving you a major scoop. You, personally, will be the first to reveal what exactly is happening at Badshah Industries. You have my word.'

'How much time?' she asked as she folded her notebook and put it back in her bag.

'I can't say. Just put your editor off. Tell him he's better off waiting instead of reporting baseless speculation.' I was proud of how I was handling all of it.

'Okay,' she said quietly. She took another sip of her drink. 'I'll see what I can do.'

'Now,' I said to her. 'Tell me everything you know about Kismet Corp. in New Jersey.'

FIFTEEN

I called Milan as soon as Manjuli left. He was on his way to Imagine at the Atria Mall, as if he needed any more gizmos. He asked me to meet him there.

'You did *what*?' he asked as he checked out an iPod. I was telling him about my meeting with the reporter, my agreement with her.

'Just listen,' I said to him, testily, trying to make myself heard above the din in the store. 'She wanted some information from me – about what was happening with the business. I didn't give it to her. But I said I would. Once she gave me what I wanted.'

'And what was that?' he asked, putting the iPod down to focus on me.

'I wanted to know about the deal that went sour between us and Jag's dad.'

Milan sighed audibly and turned his attention towards a MacBook.

'Why can't you just let that go, Soh?' he said.

'It's finished between you and that dude. Anything you find out is not going to bring him back.'

I knew Milan was right – too much had gone wrong between Jag and me, at least in Milan's estimation – for it ever to be righted. But that didn't negate my need for the truth. I started to cry.

'Oh crap, stop it,' Milan said, shoving his hands in his pocket for a clean tissue. All he found was a crumpled paper napkin from The Coffee Bean & Tea Leaf. He handed it over.

'They'll bill us for tear-soaked hard drives, and then you and I will really get it in the neck from Baba,' he said.

'Okay, so, fine, what did you learn?' He had pulled me to one side, away from the other shoppers.

'It's Amit Uncle,' I said quietly. 'He was behind the deal that went wrong. He promised Jag's dad that he and other investors from here would share in the redevelopment project if Balu Sachdev acquired a large plot of land. He did, for millions and millions of dollars. But then the property market tanked. Amit Uncle changed his mind. He left Jag's dad holding a mortgage on land he couldn't sell. And now he can't find any other investors.'

'Oops,' said Milan.

'Really? "Oops"? That's all you can say?'

'It's business, Soh. It happens every day. People change their minds. They need to get out of deals. Circumstances change. The problem here is that your guy Jag doesn't know everything. He only heard his father's side of it.'

'What else is there to know?' I asked Milan, irritated at how cavalier he was being. 'A promise was made, and then it was broken. And because Amit Uncle went back on his word to Balu Sachdev, Jag went back on his word to me.'

PART TWO

SIXTEEN

Baba had an older brother, known simply as Matunga Dada because he lived in that particular precinct of Mumbai.

Where Baba was stern and aloof, his brother was charismatic and warm-hearted. He wore thick-rimmed glasses, still dyed his hair black, and covered his gaunt frame with a bright green shawl crocheted by his late wife and presented to him on their honeymoon. It was moth-eaten, itchy to the touch, but it almost never left his body.

Matunga Dada was, in Baba's words, 'a failure in life'. He was retired from his job as a manager in a small company exporting silver trinkets. He had been widowed for years. He had no children and lived alone in a rickety walk-up opposite a street-side barber shop and above a paan-wala. It had been his home for decades, long after his younger brother had moved on to mansions and Machiavellian business deals.

Of everyone in the family, I was the one who visited Matunga Dada the most. Baba and he barely spoke. My mother would visit a few times a year, sometimes accompanied by my aunts, Malini griping about her Louboutin heels getting stuck in the worn wooden steps leading up to the third-floor flat. Inside, she would stare in horror at the stained woollen throw covering the couch and the odd cockroach that scurried behind the rabbit-eared television. Only Preeti Chachi shared my fondness for Matunga Dada. She always touched his feet and brought him cashew mithai from Mishty Bela in Walkeshwar.

Often, I went on my own to see him. I never needed a reason or an appointment – he was always home, and delighted to see me, and would press my head to his thin chest to show his appreciation. Perhaps intuiting that I was a perennially heartbroken and emotionally dependent twenty-six-year-old who always seemed to pick the wrong men, he called me 'baby'.

I showed up that afternoon holding a tin of chocolate-dipped cookies. I had awoken that morning thinking of him. It had been a week since Baba had announced to the family his plans for the company and I still felt unsteady. Even though Matunga Dada was as far removed from the workings of corporate Mumbai as it was possible to be, I felt a pull to sit in his presence.

'Baby, come in,' he said. 'So happy you're here. You are my favourite grandniece.'

'I am your *only* grandniece,' I said, smiling.

'That's why you're my favourite,' he said. We always had the exact same exchange, and it never got old.

'To what do I owe the pleasure, my dear?' he asked, ushering me to the couch. He aspired to speak like a character in one of the BBC productions he liked watching. An old Olympus typewriter rested on a table in front of the couch, a half-completed envelope inside its roller. I didn't even think one could buy typewriter ribbons any more, until I realized that Dada probably had a cache of them. He was an inveterate hoarder.

'Just thinking of you, Dada. I wanted to make sure you were okay.'

He gazed at me. I could see myself reflected in his rainbow-hued spectacle lenses.

'Things are changing, no?' he said. Even though he was isolated in so many ways, he still heard things.

'Yes, a lot. Everyone tells me not to worry. That I should get married, make a life of my own.'

'Has a good boy stolen your heart?' he asked, smiling. I loved his old-fashioned charm.

'Sadly, no,' I said.

After Jag, my love life had been depressingly non-existent. There had been the debonair visiting chef from Rio de Janeiro at the Oberoi who had plied me with caipirinhas, captivated me with delectable pao de queijos and invited me up to his suite, ostensibly to feed me some deep-fried bananas. I had declined.

Milan had enthusiastically encouraged me to flit from one fling to the next, introducing me to a friend who was an emerging fashion designer and who wanted me to be his muse, but who insisted on seeing me naked first. But these sorties felt forced. With my heart still aching for Jag, celibacy felt like the safest option. No man could possibly match him.

Now, Dada arose from the seat opposite mine and came to sit next to me.

'What is troubling you, baby?' he asked.

I hadn't planned on saying anything about what was happening in the family. But Matunga Dada had a way of making me feel safe and understood.

'I don't get Baba,' I said. 'Why he's treating his own sons like this and making the grandsons fight over a business they all should be sharing. It seems so … cruel.'

Dada lowered his head, scratched the back

of his neck. In his mid-eighties, his mind was as agile as that of a man half his age.

'There are things about my brother that people will never know,' he said. 'If they did, they would understand him better. He is a mystery. You are concerned about the family, and that is because you are a good girl. But all of you will survive this. Now, please excuse me for a moment, Sohana. I am an old man. The bathroom is my most visited room.' He laughed, stood up, disappeared behind a door. A young servant boy came in, a soiled dish rag over his shoulders, and laid out tea and the biscuits I had brought. He bowed slightly and left.

My eye fell upon a framed photograph in a cabinet, one I'd never noticed before. I walked over to it, opened the cabinet door and pulled it out. It was a black-and-white picture of Baba on his wedding day, at a rented college dining hall in Churchgate, seated on a chair next to his bride. In an era when love marriages were rare, his wife had fought to have one. According to what I'd been told growing up, she had married down; her family was wealthy, thoroughbred. Her father had been given a Rai Bahadur, and Baba was only, by then, a manager in a steel mill, from a small family in Matunga.

In the picture, he was in a dark suit and tie, his face earnest, his black shoes polished to a gleam. Dadi wore a pale, lightly embroidered sari. Around her neck was a slender diamond necklace. She wasn't touching her husband, wasn't even looking at him, and was staring sombrely into the camera instead. Had the wedding been today, it would have been held in Istanbul or Prague, and she would have worn rose-cut diamonds and a Sabyasachi lehenga, the cost of which could have fed a small village in UP for a year. She would have smooched her new husband for the battalion of cameras in front of her, her virtue slackened by Veuve Clicquot.

It wasn't surprising that Baba and Dadi had remained married for fifty-five years and stayed together against all odds. Their union had been simple, fundamental. They lived to make each other happy.

I reached back inside the cabinet to replace the framed photo. But before I put it down, my eye fell upon a scroll that extended to half the length of the shelf; it was tied with coarse twine. Almost acting of its own volition, my hand grabbed the roll of paper and freed it from its dust-covered perch, taking care not to topple the small porcelain figurines that shielded it. I tugged at the twine till it came loose in my hands, and unfurled the paper that crackled like thin skin. In smudged blue ink at the bottom was a date,

1945. The rest of the contents were gibberish:
diagrams and equations and notations, a large
concave outline shaded in charcoal, tiny figures
pencilled in around its periphery.

'So you've found my treasure, have you?'

I jumped, clutched my heart.

'Dada ... I'm sorry ... I didn't hear you coming.'
I realized that was a stupid thing to say.

'That's okay,' he said, taking the paper from my
hands and rolling it up again. 'I had forgotten
this was there.'

'What is it?' I asked.

I put my arm through his, led him back to the
couch and sat him down. A few flies had landed
on the cookies. I pushed the plate away.

'Nothing at all. Simply an idea I had. When I
was a young and foolish boy.'

'It looked interesting,' I said. 'Detailed. Like a
lot of thought had been put into it.'

'I had quite an engineering mind, back in the
day. Before I went to do the books for a company
selling silver payals.' He smiled. 'I came up with an
idea for a tool to be used in steel mills. Darshan
was working in one. Things were very basic. The
thing you saw, it was a pulley. Something to
expedite production. I just dreamed it up.'

'What happened to the idea?' I asked. 'Did
anyone else ever see it?'

'My brother did.' Dada leaned back against the couch, rested his spider-veined hands on his creased white kurta. 'He saw it. And then, years later, when he opened his first steel mill, he took it.'

'What do you mean, he took it?'

'He took it, developed it, used it in the mills. It became a standard in the industry. But he started it.'

'*You* started it.' I corrected him. 'It was *your* idea, *your* invention.' I looked around the room. Dada's entire flat could fit into Baba's bedroom. There were no cockroaches in Baba's house, no flies landing on tinned chocolate cookies and no soiled dish rags. In Baba's house, everything was pristine.

Dada leaned forward in his chair and took my hands in his.

'I need my rest, sweet girl. You go now.'

SEVENTEEN

The injustice of what seemed to have transpired – an idea hatched decades ago by one brother and then stolen by the other – stayed with me for days afterwards. The more I thought of Matunga Dada – his trusting nature, the large, sad eyes reflected through his thick lenses, the veil of loneliness that fell upon his every move, his every breath – the more I began to resent my own grandfather. If I didn't love Baba as much as I did, I would have hated him.

'So Baba ripped off some invention?' Milan asked, pouring me an espresso from a sleek black machine. 'So what? There's no such thing as an original idea anyway.'

'When did you become such a cynic?' I settled into a chair across from Milan's desk, which was so large that it took up most of the small space. The door to his office carried a brown-and-gold sign that said 'Vertex' under which, in almost indiscernible print, were the words, 'A Subsidiary of Badshah Industries'. That was not entirely true. The only thing that Vertex had to do with Badshah was that Milan happened to be one. Baba had some vague notion that Milan had set up a small office in Prabhadevi but had no idea what happened in it, nor did he care. If it didn't contribute anything to the family coffers, then it was of no consequence – although now that Milan had declared himself to be in the running to take over the family business, I wondered if that would change.

But Milan, unlike most of his cousins, didn't really give a toss about what Baba thought of his activities. Like the rest of us, he collected a nice monthly stipend simply for being a Badshah. But he was also remarkably enterprising. He had become a robust day trader, divining the movements of the stock market like a seasoned pro, rattling off facts and figures about IPOs as if he were some Wall Street kingpin. He would talk about shorting and selling with the same expertise that I displayed when speaking about seaweed body wraps and Dolce & Gabbana's fall collection. I had no idea what he babbled on about, but knew only that, on his own, he was making a significant amount of money every month. He was a silent partner in half-a-dozen other businesses, including an animation studio in Chennai, a restaurant in Bangalore and a boutique hotel in Kerala. He was the most rebellious and unconventional of all the grandchildren; he was also, ironically, the one who most closely mirrored Baba's ambition in his own early days.

'So, what have you got for me?' Milan asked now. He leaned back in his chair, causing it to squeak softly, and stretched his legs out so they rested on the table. I was staring straight at the soles of his limited edition Adidas sneakers. He had texted me early in the morning, asking me to come by his office to brainstorm business ideas.

'I wrote down a few thoughts,' I said while I rifled through my purse for my small notebook.

'If they have anything to do with clothes, bags or spa treatments, I'm not interested,' he said. 'Like this town needs any more goddamn designer boutiques and expensive massages.'

'Of course,' I said, shaking my head. 'I'm not that stupid.' I glanced down at an inside page of the notebook. The first line read 'Harvey Nichols Mumbai?' Under that, 'Medi-Spa chain – full range of face and body services, Beverly Hills-style'. Number three on my list of genius business ideas: 'Personal shopping/wardrobe consultant/personal stylist, great for Bollywood stars'.

Didn't everybody always say, 'Do what you

know best?' I *knew* this stuff. I had thought that Milan would leap out of his chair and hug me. Evidently that wasn't going to happen.

'So, what then?' he asked. He folded his hands behind his head and gazed squarely at me. 'I was hoping you'd come in hot, give me something we could run with, something so new and brilliant it'll piss everyone else off.'

I searched in every foggy crevice of my mind. Clearly, an outside-the-box thinker I was not. I tried to recall all those late-night conversations with Jag when he spoke excitedly about one earth-saving, money making prospect or the other. I forced my eyes shut: could I not remember *anything*?

'Oh, got it!' I said. 'Recycling centres. Selling scrap aluminium, glass and plastic to third-party buyers. There is potential for consistent monthly revenue.' I smiled to myself in satisfaction, impressed at how savvy I sounded. It was all coming back to me now. Jag's company had been involved in setting up such centres around northern California. In fact, there were grants awarded to the owners. He liked it because there was always a decent profit margin, and something helpful was being done for the environment at the same time.

'What?' Milan asked. 'What are you blathering on about?'

He lifted his legs off the table and tucked them under the desk.

'Sohana, take a look around you. All of Mumbai is a recycling centre. People dump their crap anywhere they can, and other people come along and use it. It's a perfect system. So I'm going to say "no".'

He turned his attention to his computer screen, plucked the keyboard off his desk, placed it on his lap and started typing, ignoring me.

'Why are you doing this?' I asked.

'Doing what?' he replied, only half-listening.

'Trying to come up with a new business angle for Baba. To win the company. Why do you care? Let Sharan and Karan fight over it. You've got your own thing going here. You're happy. Right?'

'Actually no, I'm not,' he said. 'Not happy enough. Why should I stop at this when I've got worlds to conquer? It irritates me that Sharan thinks he can just waltz in and take the company. He might be our cousin, but he's a jackass. I want to put him in his place. And I want you to help me do it. But that's not going to happen if you keep coming up with dumb ideas.'

He went back to tapping on his keyboard.

This was the one thing I hated about Milan – the way he shut me out, talked down to me. He was the closest person to me in my family, closer even than my own brothers. As kids, playing hide-and-seek in Baba's house, he and I always teamed up, his hand over my mouth to prevent me from giggling as we hid ourselves in a darkened closet while the other cousins came searching for us. We had always been inseparable.

'You're not being fair, Milan,' I said quietly. He was my best friend and, right now especially, I needed him to be kind to me. 'I'm not a business person, you know that. I don't have a clue about any of it.'

He stood up, came around to my side of the table and leaned against its edge.

'Soh, you're much more than you think you are,' he said. In his pocket, his phone rang, lighting up with a Cee Lo Green song. He ignored it. 'You have to start thinking like a business person. It's in your genes. You're a Badshah. A born wheeler-dealer. How many times have you walked into a restaurant, taken one look at the ambience and the crowd, and known if it was going to fail or succeed? I've seen you stare at a bare plot of land and imagine a block of flats there, what colour the building should be, how you would market it. I've heard you talk like that a hundred times. Giving people what they want, what they will pay for – that's business. You already know this stuff, without even knowing that you know it.'

In all of Milan's twenty-five years, it was the kindest, most encouraging thing he'd ever said to me.

'Come on,' he said, grabbing his keys out of a desk drawer. 'Let's get out of here. It's cocktail hour.'

I glanced at my watch. 'Milan, it's eleven in the morning.'

He smiled impishly, raised an eyebrow. 'Exactly.'

'Everything has become a secret,' Milan said. We were at the Harbour Bar at the Taj and he was on his second martini. That the wait staff barely acknowledged the ridiculousness of such a deranged order in the middle of the morning said more about Mumbai society's drinking habits than anything else.

'What do you mean?' I asked. I had stuck to tea. The more alcohol I drank, the more emotional I became, and I was sufficiently unhinged as it was.

'Like my brother. After what Baba said, he's holed up in his room at home. I hear him on the phone. I see him drawing up plans. I have no idea what he's up to and it's driving me crazy.'

'Why?' I asked. 'Because you know it's going to be good?'

He picked up a toothpick speared with an olive and grasped it between his teeth.

'He's a smart boy, that Pawan. Smarter than me. That's why I need you to help me.'

'What do you want me to do?'

'Spy on him.'

'I can't do that.'

'Sure you can. Just find out what he's up to. Knowledge is power, you know.'

This was it. Everything I had feared. Cousin against cousin, brother against brother. This family was getting seedier by the day. Lawsuits. Accusations. In-fighting. And now, espionage. It was horrible. I wanted no part in it.

'I can't, Milan,' I said quietly. 'I'll do anything for you, you know that. But I don't want to get dragged into this.'

'You have to, Soh,' he said. 'If you have ever given a damn about me, you have to do this. I need to know what the hell is going on with everybody else so I can beat it …' Then he added, 'There's something else. If Sharan or Karan take over, there's no saying what they'll do with the dads. Those cousins of ours can be bastards. But if I'm in control, I'll make sure your dad always has his place there.'

I stared across the table at my cousin, the only person in my family who knew about Jag, who let me cry on his shoulder when I had returned home. The only one now who seemed to sense what frightened me the most about the whole affair: that my father would lose his place in his own world.

Milan was right. I couldn't refuse. As much as I railed against the idea of taking sides, I had just picked one.

EIGHTEEN

Even though I had nodded in agreement when Milan had asked me to be his 'spy', the prospect played on my mind for days. It was my first ever real crisis of conscience, and it unnerved me. Although I wasn't especially close to Sharan, Karan or Pawan, they were still my cousins, bound to me by blood the same way that Milan was.

As I had expected, Baba's decree had sent all the cousins, except Armaan, scurrying off into their respective corners, each one weaving plans that no one else was going to be privy to until they were ready to be presented.

While I had never exactly had a cosy familiarity with the inner workings of the Badshah empire, I was at least moderately aware of a framework: the times that Sharan had been to Silicon Valley, I was vaguely cognizant of an IT company he went to check out to invest in. Those trips that Karan made to Abu Dhabi had something to do with commercial real estate. Pawan, soon after he had returned from college, had gone to work for Baba for a year, and in that time had been sent on a recon mission to South Africa to determine the viability of the retail landscape. Pawan had left the Badshah employ because, or so he said, his 'needs weren't being met', although he never specified what those needs were. Now he spent his days tutoring kids on engineering, showing them how to build small mechanical robots and tanks and solar-powered toy cars.

Still, whatever transparency there had been within the family in the past was now gone. The whole thing was infuriating and divisive, and left everyone edgier than usual at family get-togethers.

'How am I going to do this?' I asked Milan on the phone. He was in his car, stalled in a dead sea of rush-hour traffic. 'How am I going to get the information for you? And what happens if everyone finds out I'm snooping?'

'Firstly, that won't happen,' he said. A cacophony of honks erupted around him. 'They'll never know my info came from you. All you have to do is keep your ears open, be your charming self. They'll tell you stuff. You pose no threat. You're harmless.'

Nonetheless, I needed a plan. As much of

a bubblehead as my cousins thought I was, I could hardly sidle up to them and start asking questions about what they were up to, when I had never done so before. I needed to develop street smarts, to come up with a strategy. I knew it was wrong, almost reprehensible, but I shrugged off the guilt that had afflicted me. I was too deep in it anyway by now.

'Hi Jaanvi, want to have lunch?'

My cousin-in-law went silent. In the three years that she had been married to Sharan, I had never taken any time out to call her and invite her anywhere.

'Is everything okay?' she asked, understandably.

'Oh, everything's perfect. I just thought that, you know, it might be nice for us to get together and talk, what with everything going on.'

To my own ears, I sounded sincere, perhaps because there *was* a vestige of authenticity to what I was saying, though inside I felt disgraceful. I should have worked on knowing her better from the very beginning.

'It's very nice of you,' she said. I heard her flicking through the pages of a diary.

'I'm free this Wednesday,' she said. 'Where would you like to go?'

We ended up lunching at the home she shared with Sharan, Karan and her in-laws. It was a penthouse in Worli, two floors broken to create one duplex, its interiors an elegant mix of sea-foam green and a luminous shade of clotted cream. She greeted me in black jeans and clogs, rudraksha beads around her neck.

'I hope you didn't mind coming here,' she said. 'I thought, what's the point of dealing with all that hideous traffic? We'll be much more comfortable at home.' She hugged me stiffly. 'Mamma's out, so it's just us.'

She led me into the living room, whisper-quiet and immaculate. A maid came in, asking what I'd like to drink. Lunch was already set in the dining room, the silver chafing dishes brilliant against the glossy mahogany table.

'So, tell me,' she said. 'How is everything?' She pushed her hair back behind an ear and spooned aloo mattar and rogan josh onto my plate.

She was nice to a fault, obliging, benevolent. I felt a shadow of remorse for the times I had made fun of her, had laughed at Milan's jokes at her expense. I saw now that Sharan was not worthy of her. None of us were.

'I've just been feeling a bit wrecked about everything,' I said. For a moment, I forgot why I was really there – to pry information out of this kind and unsuspecting woman. Then I was suddenly filled with shame.

'Yes, it's been difficult,' she said. Her accent was bracing, English, the result of her years at a British boarding school while her father made millions in West Africa.

'You know, that night, after Baba made his speech to all of us … things were horrible at home,' she said. 'Mamma ranted for two hours. Sharan was furious.'

Something had rearranged itself. She was sharing a confidence, talking to me like an ally.

'I can imagine,' I said. 'He probably figured everything would be his. And now, he has to fight for it. What do you think he's going to do?' I asked. 'Does he have any grand plans?' I hoped I wasn't being too obvious.

'If he did, I wouldn't know of them,' she replied. She pushed grains of fluffy white rice around on her plate. 'He doesn't really tell me much. He talks to his mother more. And to Mary, of course. His assistant. She's been helping him with whatever he's working on. But I did hear him on the phone the other night, arguing with someone.'

'Oh? What was going on?' I had to be careful about the inflection in my voice.

'No idea,' she said. 'Something about cold

fusion. That's what he kept saying, over and over.'

'Cold fusion?' I repeated. 'What is that? Like some frozen yogurt franchise?'

Jaanvi smiled.

'I think it's a bit more complicated than that,' she said.

'Oh well, I'm sure he knows what he's doing,' I said, dismissing the subject. I needed to move on to something more everyday, more innocent. Whatever she had revealed to me would have to do for now.

NINETEEN

As I discovered, one of the perks of belonging to a newly outed wealthy family is access to just about anything. Seats on fully booked flights become mysteriously available. Lines outside hot nightclubs shift to one side as the rich girl and her posse make their way to the front. Maître d's march towards the best table in the house, helping the rich usurp space that others were poised to occupy. It is a mythic way to live, shielded from life's everyday inconveniences, its commonplace letdowns.

Being a Badshah had come with its drawbacks, the most painful of which was losing Jag. So I decided, at the grand age of twenty-six, that I was going to start taking full advantage of the circumstance of my birth too.

And everything that had happened recently made me think about what I could do to be better, more interesting, more accomplished.

Jag, a busy and evolved man with a demanding

career, knew how to steam artichokes, gut fresh trout and blanch almonds. I, on the other hand, burned water.

So I decided to finally live up to my promise to Jag that I would eventually learn how to take care of myself in the most basic way, even if he was no longer around to see it.

Through a friend who was high up enough at the JW Marriott Hotel, I scored private lessons with a sous chef there, a short, moustachioed man whose toque sat loosely on his head and who looked rather offended at being asked, on his afternoon off, to do something as demeaning as teaching a socialite how to toast cumin seeds.

'What is this for?' he asked me during our first lesson, handing over a mortar and pestle so I could start pounding some poor garlic cloves. 'Did you win a prize?'

'No, I just want to learn a few basic dishes.'

'There are plenty of cookery schools in Mumbai,' he replied, fingering fragments of translucent garlic skin out of the granite bowl. 'Why you don't watch *Khana Khazana*? I'm thinking that that Sanjeev Kapoor is used to dealing with people who don't know what they are doing.'

'Please, sir,' I said. I realized I didn't even know the man's name. No wonder he was already put off by me; I had walked in like some entitled diva, clueless, desperate, a phony with a designer handbag.

'I just really, really want to learn. I hear you're one of the best.' I looked straight into his tiny eyes. 'Whatever you can teach me. Please. I promise I won't let you down.'

After three hours of dicing, slicing, sautéing and learning not to run in the opposite direction when the pressure cooker whistled, I felt the stirrings of a cook in me. As I took off my apron, Chef Daaruk said the words I never thought he'd say to me: 'Same time next week?'

Six lessons and eighteen hours of practice later, I felt confident enough to host my first ever solo dinner party. With Chef – that was what he wanted me to call him – we planned the menu, down to the most inconsequential pickled condiment. I prepared a guest list – eight would be the perfect number, just enough to comfortably occupy the formal dining table. I even brought my set of calligraphy pens out of retirement. I wrote out invitations on light golden stock paper and had them hand-delivered by the driver, who looked at me as if to ask, 'I'm spending six hours in traffic to drop off invitations to a *dinner party*?' However, he wiggled his head in quiet acquiescence and left, perhaps taking consolation from the fact that he now had the opportunity to spend the afternoon alone behind the wheel of an air-conditioned luxury car, playing whatever CD as suited his fancy.

I informed my family that I would require sole use of the apartment that night. Then I handed Chanoo an extensive list of ingredients and she twitched nervously, clearly wondering what lunacy had struck me. The last time I had entered the kitchen had been to find a spoon, and I had needed directions even for that.

On the warm, wet Saturday morning of my soirée, I briskly commandeered the kitchen, a glossy pink folder stuffed with scribbled notes and dog-eared recipes tucked under my arm. Chanoo, more weakly this time, asked me again to leave everything to her and the staff, to go and enjoy my day like I always did.

'Relax,' she said, her face taking on a combination of concern and profound scepticism. 'Let *us* do this. It is *our* job.'

I put the folder down on the counter, placed a hand on her wiry arm, and uttered the words – in an incomprehensible (to her) English – that Jag used to say to me all the time.

'I've got this.'

Minutes before my guests arrived, I stepped back and gazed at the elegance of my table. A deep burgundy linen tablecloth, topped with gleaming gold-plated cutlery, bronze-coloured square dishes, a row of tapered candles set atop an embroidered brocade runner. Arranging who would sit where had taken all the strategy of launching a military strike, and I hoped that none of my guests would fall prey to the Mumbai proclivity – something I had been guilty of a few times too many – of bailing because a better offer had come up. That would throw everything out of whack, and I needed the night to be perfect. I needed to show my family and the throng of people who ran our lives that I wasn't just some well-intentioned bimbette, that I could do *something*.

I went into the kitchen to check on the food, which lay ready to be plated as soon as we moved into the dining room. On Chef's recommendation, I had gone with an Indo-fusion theme. My mentor had even delved into his personal stash of gourmet acquisitions to help me, generously handing over a bottle of boysenberry vinaigrette acquired on a trip to Sweden and parting with a Quinta do Noval from Portugal to serve with dessert. The eggplant chips with tamarind date sauce were crisp and ready for the guests to nibble at with the cocktails, the herbed pine nut brittle was expertly laid out adjacent to a verdant salad, the chicken makhni lay simmering next to the bowl of cashew pesto which was to be ladled on right before serving. It was deceptively simple.

I gazed at the feast I had prepared, largely on my own, and felt prouder of the accomplishment than anything I'd ever done in my life.

The doorbell rang and I raced to the door, cutting off Chanoo as she reached for the handle. Nitya was the first one, uncommonly early, gorgeous in an emerald-green Dior with a pouf skirt. She had an enviable wardrobe, one that was not the result of her yoga studio business. Nitya, like so many of us, had a lifestyle that was subsidized by her father's money. Without him, she would never have been able to afford even half of what she owned.

'What a treat, a dinner party for no reason,' she said, leaning forward to kiss me on both cheeks, and walked past me, straight into the living room.

'So, who else is coming?' she asked, plucking a glass of champagne off a tray offered to her.

'Don't worry, you'll know everyone here,' I said.

'Oh, that's a disappointment. I was hoping to meet some new people. Some new *guys*, preferably.'

'Sorry, can't help there,' I said.

She sat down, crossed her legs. 'So, heard from your American boyfriend?' she asked.

'His name is Jag. He's not my boyfriend anymore. And if I'd heard from him, don't you think you'd know?'

'Someone's cranky,' she said, downing the rest of her drink and reaching out for a skewer of lamb koftas. She took a big bite.

'Mmm, these are good.' She examined them closely, as if searching for the recipe within the meat.

'Oh, I'm so glad you like them. I used scallions, semolina, a touch of allspice. Interesting flavour, right?'

'*You* made these?' she asked, putting the half-eaten skewer down on a cocktail platter. 'I thought it was something fancy dreamed up by that cook of yours.'

'I've made everything you'll be eating tonight,' I said, proudly. 'That's the point. I've been taking lessons and wanted to treat my friends to a formal home-cooked meal.'

'Well, darling, that's a lovely thought, but I do hope you have some Pudin Hara handy.' She laughed a shrill, abrasive laugh, like an early version of Malini. Malini 1.0.

I was grateful when the doorbell rang again. It was Milan and Pawan, the latter still looking perplexed that I had invited him. They were the only two family members who had made it to the guest list.

'What's *she* doing here?' Milan asked, peering through the foyer into the living room at Nitya. 'I was hoping this was going to be a psycho-free zone.'

'She's my best friend,' I whispered. 'How could I not invite her?'

He rolled his eyes, followed me in.

Everyone else arrived within forty minutes, surely a record in a city in which dinner parties routinely began at eleven.

Milan looked at the champagne. 'You know, Soh, you're better off serving vodka,' he said, quietly. 'It gives you a great hit without making you sleepy.'

'I love how we're having a conversation about how to get the best buzz,' I said. 'Our mothers would be so proud.'

My friend Jaya came in along with her husband, Kaushik.

'This is so lovely, Sohana,' she said, and Kaushik nodded in agreement. They were

Mumbai's ultimate power couple; he the founder of a tech firm that was on the cusp of its first IPO, she the owner of a public relations firm that represented the world's biggest luxury brands in India. Despite their success and their individual high profiles, there was something folksy and endearing about them. Three children at home, a loving relationship, every imaginable professional accomplishment – Jaya was the person I wanted to be when I finally grew up.

Then there was Pancho, a good friend of Milan's who was recovering from a vicious divorce that had been accelerated by the discomfiting fact that, after four years of trying manically to have a baby, and numerous embarrassing tests, Pancho discovered his wife to have been on the Pill the entire time. Milan had told me that Pancho wanted to date again. Now, as I sat looking at him, the beaten-down boy who needed to be loved, I wondered if maybe he – with his designer stubble and rough-hewn charisma – and Nitya might hit it off. They had met a couple of times socially, but never had the chance to really talk. Perhaps the dinner party would change that.

But nothing could quite compare to the arrival of Anushka. She and I were in a nascent stage of friendship, having chatted briefly at parties. She was a stage actress in Toronto, a budding

Bollywoodite in India, and was willowy, glowing, with an impeccable sense of style and an uncanny ability to court just the right amount of harmless scandal and pointless speculation – enough to keep her in the public eye, but not so much as to besmirch her name. At dinner, she was seated opposite Pawan, who managed the difficult task of feeding himself while keeping his eyes firmly fixed on her cleavage. Even in a black silk kurta, a burnished copper choker at her neck, her eyes smudged with kohl, and not a designer logo in sight, she was by far the most striking woman in the room. I could see Nitya almost spontaneously combust due to envy.

'Sohana, the food is really something,' said Kaushik, taking another bite of a creamy cumin-spiced risotto. 'I didn't know you could cook.'

'I couldn't,' I replied.

Nitya's plate was still full, the various dishes coalescing in the centre like discards at some unimpressive buffet.

'Is everything okay, Nitya?' I asked, indicating towards her plate. 'You've hardly touched your food.'

'It's not to my taste,' she said, bringing her hand to her chest in an act of faux contrition. 'But, please,' she continued, gesturing to the group as if she were a saint in a room full of convicts, 'everyone carry on. I'll fix myself an omelette at home.'

I felt my spirit collapse, my confidence evaporate. What hold did this girl have over me? And why did I care so much when she was the only person at the table who didn't appreciate me for what I'd done? She had just been unforgivably rude. How many people went to a dinner party and told the host they hated the food? Could she not have faked it, just a little?

'So, people, I *must* tell you about what happened at a table reading last week with Hrithik,' Anushka said. Her voice was lyrical, captivating, her manner upbeat. Heads swivelled in her direction. She had cut through the tension by remembering a key fact of Mumbai society life: everyone loved a bit of movie star gossip, that it could always be counted on to save the day. Pawan continued gazing at her. I had never seen him smitten before, and felt a pang of anguish on his behalf at the hopelessness of it.

Everyone rose for the dessert wine and Parisian lavender-scented chocolates that had been laid out in the living room.

Kaushik and Jaya said their goodbyes, wanting to go home to their children. Nitya asked if she could linger in the dining room to make a phone call. I told the servants to give her some privacy before going in to clear the table. Pancho poured a glass of pink-hued sweet wine for Anushka, eyeing the legs encased in skinny black pants and the hint of a black lace bra visible through her partially unbuttoned kurta.

It must be nice to be coveted by so many men, I thought. It was not an experience I could relate to. She was on the couch next to Pawan, who inched closer to her every time he reached forward to pick a nugget of chocolate from the table. He was telling her about an Italian art-house movie he had watched on a trip to New York. He had since purchased the DVD. He had it at home. She would love it, he insisted. Maybe she could come over and they could watch it some time?

Anushka swiftly changed the subject, talking about the last ski trip she had gone on near her home in Canada with her older brother. She missed her family in Toronto, and especially the Afghan hound she had rescued from a local animal shelter.

'I have pictures on my phone,' she announced brightly; she felt around on the sofa behind her, looked under the cushions.

'Wait. Where's my purse?' she asked.

'I think I saw it in the dining room,' said Pawan, ever vigilant about the most inconsequential of things. He looked satisfied with himself, as if he had rescued her from a burning building. Anushka stood up and began walking towards the dining room.

'Sit,' I said. 'I'll go get it.'

The double doors to the dining room were closed, in deference to Nitya's stated need for privacy. She'd sure been on the phone a long time. I pushed one door open gingerly, not wanting to interrupt her call.

I stood at the entrance. Nitya's back was to me. She wasn't on the phone. She was seated on the carved wooden arm of a dining chair, holding a plate and shovelling food into her mouth.

She put down the plate, picked up one of the serving bowls and began eating again. Then she grabbed a napkin and mopped off the gravy around her mouth.

She turned around and saw me standing there.

'Shit, Sohana, you scared me,' she said. 'What are you doing?'

'You said you hated the food,' I said.

'I was hungry. I thought it at least polite to stay here and finish my plate.'

'Yes. And the leftovers.'

Her cheeks reddened.

'Why have you been doing this?' I asked. I moved closer to her, not thinking to shut the doors behind me.

'Doing what?' She turned her body away from me defensively, looking for an escape. There wasn't one.

'Going out of your way to make me feel bad. You wanted me to think I was a crappy cook, that this experiment was a disaster. Then you sneak back in here to eat everything. What the hell is going on with you?'

A flinty, fragile silence filled the space between us. She stared at me coldly. For a moment, I didn't know who she was. Soreness swept through my body. In the dark, cold rush that followed, I remembered all the ways in which my best friend had systematically tried to crush my happiness of late, had slapped me with one hand while soothing me with the other. I couldn't remember the last time she had truly been a friend to me. It was months ago, before London.

'Answer me, Nitya.' I had moved forward and was standing just inches from her. My fingers were around her upper arm. 'You were never like this. We used to be close. I wanted you here tonight, to see what I had done. Why couldn't you just let me have this?'

'Let you have it?' Her voice shook. 'What, like you don't have enough? Being popular? Having more money than Lakshmi is permitted to bestow on a single family? Worldwide fame after what that newspaper wrote? "The lone heiress, Sohana Badshah." Well, aren't *you* something? And now you want to be a fancy cook as well. Has it ever occurred to you that maybe you're not *allowed* that much in one lifetime?'

She flung her words at me like tiny silver knives in a carnival trick.

I heard a rustling at the far end of the room. The rest of the group was standing there, staring at us. I didn't know how long everyone had been there or how much they had heard. Pancho was puffing on a cigar, looking as if he were seated in the front row at a cabaret show.

'Ooh, catfight,' said Milan.

'Go away,' I said.

'Come, boys,' Anushka trilled, leading the three of them away like a nursery school teacher would her charges. 'Someone show me the view around here.'

The diversion had provided a moment of respite. Nitya gathered herself, took a breath. Her eyes were tired. A grey pallor came over her face. She looked diminished and finally sank into a chair.

'My father lost everything in a ponzi scheme in the States,' she said quietly. 'When I say everything, I mean *everything*. He hasn't been able to handle the failure. He's mostly drunk these days.'

'I'm so sorry, Nitya,' I said. I pulled up a seat so that I faced her. Our knees touched. 'When did all this happen?'

'While you were in London. I didn't want to say anything while you were away. And then when you came back, you were in your own world, crying over that Jag fellow. I was ashamed to tell you.'

'Forgive me,' I said. 'I'm sorry I haven't been a better friend … that I was too engrossed in my own life. What can I do to help?'

She shook her head. I think she just needed me to listen at that point.

'We don't have anything anymore. My mother had to sell her wedding jewellery. This dress isn't mine. I borrowed it. Everything about me is fake.'

I wrapped my arms around her.

'Not everything,' I said.

TWENTY

Charan Badshah examined himself in the bathroom mirror, trying to ascertain how many strands of silver had sprouted on his head since he checked last. Yes, the opalescent strands that now fell away from the parting in his hair and salted his adroitly shaved sideburns did lend him a dignified mystique. He had transformed from a suave bed-hopping playboy into an urbane husband, chastened by marriage.

His wife, the stoic and cultured Jaanvi, loved him, and honoured his family. Every night, she prepared him a drink of warm milk and honey, which her Ayurvedic doctor had promised would help increase her husband's sperm count. She had flown to Hong Kong to consult with a noted practitioner of Chinese medicine who had sent her back home with clear plastic bags of chasteberry, black cohosh and Siberian ginseng, assuring her that if she consumed the herbs regularly, a baby would bloom in her belly.

Of course, these were just small components of the entire equation. They had to do things the old-fashioned way as well. So three nights a week, Jaanvi slipped into one of the La Perla nightgowns that were part of her overflowing trousseau, rubbed her husband's back as he sent out the last of the day's emails, and tempted him into bed. Her entreaties worked sometimes, on other occasions they were rebuffed. Often, he was too tired, and when he was up for it, usually after he'd had a drink or two, he was elsewhere, his mind on anything but the wife who so wanted him to impregnate her.

Jaanvi, after three years of marriage, had become accustomed to her husband's emotional absence. She had married into a prominent family and had not deluded herself that the man to whom she had been wed would ever be tender, or be truly available. Their families had forged a mighty bond and for now, that was as much as she could ask for.

Sharan thought of Jaanvi, of all she had done for him, all that she put up with. He emerged from the bathroom and sat on the edge of the king-sized bed. The hotel room was cast in a soft beige light. The sun had set long ago. Given the traffic between the Grand Hyatt in Santacruz and his home, he really ought to be leaving soon.

He heard a gentle snore from under the white covers. He stretched out his arm and placed it on a pallid, naked shoulder. A black head stirred.

'Sorry, I fell asleep,' Mary said, startled. Her pink lipstick, now smudged and faded, was imprinted on the pillow covers.

'Don't apologize,' Sharan said. He lay down next to her and placed his lips near her tiny, shell-shaped ear. 'You can be here all night if you want. I need to go.'

'Can you stay with me, just this once?' She sat up in bed, let the sheets fall below her waist. She was curvy, soft and feminine, her skin like diaphanous silk. Sharan was hooked on touching her.

'Not this time. I'll have to plan it better. I don't want anyone to get suspicious.'

'By anyone, you mean *her*, right? Your wife?'

'Of course I mean her. Who else would I be talking about?' he snapped. 'I'm cheating. I'm having an affair with my secretary. If it wasn't such a cliché, it would be a joke.' He sounded sour, and rued the words as soon as they tumbled out of his mouth.

'Oh, I'm a joke now, am I?' came the retort.

Her bob was perfect, not a hair out of place, despite the amorous rough-housing that had taken place between the sheets a couple of hours earlier.

'Come on, I didn't mean that,' Sharan said. He was exhausted – tired of placating one woman here and then going home to pacify another.

She threw the blanket off, stomped into the bathroom, slammed the door.

Sharan heard the shower run. He wasn't planning to make anything better that night. He wrote a note telling Mary he would call later. Then he did what he always did: left enough cash in an envelope for her to get a taxi home. In the beginning of their affair, he would ask Mohit, his driver, to take her back. But when he realized that Mohit had come to suspect that perhaps these out-of-office sessions between his boss and the secretary were not entirely chaste, Sharan had started to make other arrangements. The envelope now on the nightstand, he slipped out of the room, impressed with his chivalry. He was nothing, after all, if not a gentleman.

Her fragrant, damp hair clinging to her head, Mary picked up her clothes that trailed the path to the hotel bed. She was grateful for the hot shower, for the firm pressure of it that soothed her shoulders. Where she lived with her parents, not far from the hotel, there was no such luxury.

Now she wriggled her frame back into Sharan's favourite lilac lacy teddy. It had been, in fact, a gift from him three months ago on the first anniversary of their affair. It was one of the very few things he had given her since their dalliance had begun and – she thought bitterly as she snapped the straps into place – one that served him more than it did her. This was Sharan to a fault. There had been no surprise flowers in the afternoon, no rainy walks in the park, no diamonds in red velvet boxes and candlelit dinners in private rooms. There was only this, a suite at the Grand Hyatt that was always booked in her name using a company credit card, the occasional piece of lingerie, a gold charm bracelet from Sharjah which she was convinced he had purchased as an afterthought at the airport (and which, as his credit card bill later proved, was an accurate suspicion). Mary knew what Jaanvi got, what Jaanvi would always get, and it burnt a hole through her heart.

Dressed in the brown skirt and polka-dotted cream top she had worn to work that morning, Mary plucked the envelope filled with cash from the nightstand. There was, as always, more than enough; it usually covered her cab ride home and allowed her a little trinket or two for herself. This time, however, she would give the extra to her mother, tell her it was a bonus for a job well done. That would not be too far from the truth.

In the back of the taxi, Mary thought of all the ways in which she made her boss' life better. She stayed with him when he worked late, returning calls, bringing him cups of decaf, rubbing his sore neck when the rest of the floor was dark and silent. When they were able to steal away for their trysts, she gave him her all. No matter how tiring her day, what her obligations to her friends or parents, she opened herself to Sharan in the most primal way, stroking his ego, unburdening his body. Jaanvi could do none of this, and was, in fact, the cement block dragging him down into a swirling black ocean of melancholy. Especially now, with his very livelihood at stake, Sharan needed someone who understood him, who wanted nothing but his happiness, his victory. She, Mary, loved him through and through. She *knew* him, was able to divine from his every look, his every inflection, what he needed.

It had started as a bit of fun, an inevitable release of the sexual tension that had excited them the moment she had entered for her interview, when Sharan had gazed at those profuse breasts, her slender waist, her pouty lips, and given her the job that dozens of far worthier applicants had applied for. But, of late, what they had wasn't fun – at least not for Mary. She needed more from Sharan. She could give him everything that his wife couldn't. She had lost her temper with him tonight, and wished she hadn't. It was not the prerogative of a mistress to make demands. But, as Mary had gradually realized, she didn't want to be her boss' mistress any more.

The taxi grovelled by at an excruciating pace. She checked her watch. At this rate, she wouldn't make it home until past ten. She heard a knock at her window – a small, grubby face trying to peer inside. Almost by instinct, she shoved her hand into her bag to seek out some change and rolled the glass pane down. The beggar boy thrust his dirt-smudged brown hand inside, and Mary gave him the detritus of currency she found remaindered in the bottom of her purse. He was about to go off, satisfied with what he had collected.

'Thehro,' she commanded and handed something else over.

The taxi trundled off.

The boy stood in the traffic, examining the contents of the white envelope the lady had given him, his eyes widening in delight at the accordion-pleats of hundred-rupee notes. But there was something else nestled in their midst, something unexpected. He pulled out a circular packet with small white pills around its circumference. There were tiny words beneath each one, words his illiterate eyes could not decipher. He popped one of the pills in his mouth, hoping for a drop of sweetness. None came. He spat it out.

In the back of the taxi, Mary felt relieved that she no longer had to hide the birth control pills – the ones that Sharan made her take, convinced that the lack of a baby in his wife's womb had nothing to do with him – from her stridently Catholic mother.

No. Between the time Sharan had left their hotel room to the time she had stepped into the cab, Mary had made a decision. She was going to be Sharan Badshah's mistress no more.

TWENTY-ONE

My dinner party – or, as Milan would come to refer to it, 'The Last Supper' – heightened my standing in the Badshah household. In the kitchen, the cook no longer flinched when I walked in.

I sent Chef Daaruk a Longines watch to thank him. He sent it back with a note that said, 'You were the one wearing the apron.'

But that evening totally transformed my friendship with Nitya. After she had cried for a few minutes that night, she went to wash up and Milan had – quite intuitively, as it turns out – pointed out: 'You guys will be best friends again now that she's gotten the crazy out of her.'

So I took her in hand, checking in on her often, but also trying to ensure that she never felt like a charity case. We put a hold on our tea drinking sessions at the Four Seasons, and our shopping excursions to Ensemble and Jimmy Choo. Instead, we decided that tea at her place was better than anywhere else because of her cook's famous toasted Kraft cheese-and-chilli sandwiches. And really, we didn't need to shop for new outfits for some late-night shindig because staying home and watching a DVD was so much more fun.

'What's happening with your family?' she asked one day. It was the first time she had posed the question in a way that I didn't construe as needling or laden with malice. I could answer without feeling defensive. We had just left a small neighbourhood temple, one that her mother took her to as a child. We were putting our shoes back on, sitting on a bench outside, its paint peeling, pigeon excrement caking its surface. It was early evening. The carefree trill of a child's laughter sounded from an adjacent building. Off to one side, two women in purdah talked loudly, weighed down by mesh bags stuffed with vegetables. Nitya liked going there on Mondays, and then going home afterwards to break her fast. We juggled shiny waxed apples and small paper cones of fragrant prasad.

'Things aren't good,' I said.

Her face conveyed sympathy; with all she had been going through, Nitya knew what it felt like when things were rocky at home.

'I'd always thought we were a close-knit family.

But now, even though we still get together, there's this unease...'

She tugged at the strap of her sandals, easing it over her toes. The evening felt clammy. A child held onto a nub of chalk, etching out a game of hopscotch on the potholed pavement. I leaned my head against the wall behind me and closed my eyes. I felt curiously at peace. This was my favourite time of the day, that magic hour between the yellow brashness of afternoon and the velvet quiet of night. Here, now, Nitya and I were just two young women in cotton churidar-kurtas, out to seek the blessings of the deities, enjoying the anonymity and grace of a quiet visit to a temple. No parties, no photographers, no jewellery, no fuss. It was a typical Mumbai evening at its finest.

We began walking to our cars.

'What are you going to do?' she asked.

'I'm helping Milan. He's kind of made me his second-in-command. He really wants the top job, and I'm going to try and help him get it.'

'What about Armaan? I would have thought that if you had to choose between a brother and a cousin, you'd choose your brother.'

'I don't think he wants it. He's got his own thing going on. He's never been that interested in Baba's business anyway.'

'So how are you going to do it?' Nitya asked.

'What?'

'How are you going to help Milan? What can you do, exactly?'

I was stumped. I couldn't exactly tell her that my cousin was making me spy on the other members of my family, and that whatever ideas I had put forth to him on my own merit had been unceremoniously labelled as 'lame'.

'I need to be his second brain,' I said. 'Or at least half-a-brain. Baba said he would give the company to the one who brought in something bold, revolutionary. Milan needs my help in figuring out what that is.'

'Well, you won't find it if you're hanging out at house parties on Pali Hill,' she said. 'You need to go out into the world. Explore. Investigate. Talk to people.' She was leaning against the back door of her car, its white exterior newly buffed.

'Oh, right. I hadn't thought of that,' I said.

'Well, think about it then.' She said goodbye and got in as her driver turned the engine on.

After this episode I realized that if I had to help my cousin, I needed to travel further afield than Colaba. So a little sojourn was called for. Somewhere where everyone was on the cutting-edge, where if you didn't innovate every day, there was something wrong with you. A place where

I could soak in the mood of the moment, get a sense of the Next Big Thing.

California.

I told Milan this, that I wanted to go on an exploratory trip to the West Coast, a place where he had gone to college and would probably know far more about than I ever would. He and I needed to go together.

He was staring at the video game – full of cartoon men with angular faces shooting down Korean bad guys – he was engrossed in. I hated Milan's obsession with this stuff, his engagement with their violence.

'Fine, go,' he said.

'Come with me.'

'No. I'm too busy.'

'You're playing Homefront on a Wednesday afternoon.'

'I've got bigger fish to fry,' he said. 'Seriously. You go. Text me what you find out, okay, babe?'

My next thought was Nitya. This had been her idea anyway. And if Milan wasn't coming, there was nobody I'd rather go with. All I had to do now was convince her.

'Come on!' I said to her. 'It'll be fun! Los Angeles is gorgeous this time of year!'

'Why Los Angeles?' she asked.

A reasonable question.

'It's California! Everything great that has ever happened in history started there. Facebook. Hollywood. All that Silicon Valley stuff I'll never understand.'

'So what are you going to do?' she asked. 'Stand on a corner in Beverly Hills and beg for ideas?'

'I'm not sure,' I said. 'But I'll know it when I see it. Just come with me. Please? As my guest?' I had wondered how I would broach that; usually, when friends went away together, they paid for themselves. Nitya was in no position to fly anywhere, but I didn't want something as inconsequential as lack of funds to prevent her from accompanying me.

'It's cool,' she said. 'I have plenty of miles.'

But I still had to get around Dadi; I told her that Nitya had been through a horrid time recently and needed to get away. There was a beautiful ashram in the Palisades, a place where Nitya and I could say a prayer for our futures, for both our families. It was all my Dadi needed to hear to nod her approval.

TWENTY-TWO

We checked into our room at Shutters on the Beach. It was all white and bright and clean, like some immaculate Cape Cod cottage that Martha Stewart might have decorated. I had never been to LA before – New York a dozen times, Atlanta for a wedding, Arizona to see the Grand Canyon when Rajan was younger. But Los Angeles was the great unknown – a city I knew only through the coverage of the Golden Globes on the television, home to Juicy Couture, the place that had given birth to Bikram Yoga, and a city where even the biggest Bollywood stars were yet to really make their names. It was here, I was convinced, that something special lay, a dollop of brilliance conceived by somebody else, that I could take back to my cousin in Mumbai and make something happen. I just had to find it.

'Are you done?' I called out to Nitya. She had been in the shower forever. Outside, women with gravity defying breasts and taut thighs roller-skated down a beach path. Men in sweat pants jogged with their dogs. Bicycles whizzed past. The air was fresh and salty, the beach free of Chowpatty-style swill. From where I was sitting, it was Utopia.

On the bed was a folder overflowing with newspaper and magazine clippings and printouts from various Internet sites. I had done my research. There were things happening in California – inventions, advancements – that I knew Milan could do something with. I leafed through the papers now. Internet TV. Hydrogen-powered cars. Tools to harvest rainwater. Virtual technology for military applications. Bio-medical engineering. It was information that had awakened my interest when I had first seen it, and I told myself that if *I* felt interested in any of it, then surely Milan would too. A few weeks ago, I didn't even know what any of it meant. And here I was now, reading the literature I had assiduously collected, trying to figure out my next step.

Nitya finally opened the door, releasing a waft of warm citrus-infused steam. She sat down next to me on the bed and peered at the clippings.

'*You* did all this?'

I nodded.

'I guess I underestimated you,' she said. 'So? Now what?'

It was a good question, and not one that I was equipped to answer. Before leaving home, I had shot off emails to some of the companies whose clippings had interested me, requesting meetings. So far, I had heard nothing back. I was a girl from Mumbai with no business experience, sitting in a $400-a-night hotel room. A week stretched out in front of me. Somehow or other, I had to make it count.

'What now?' I said, repeating her question. 'We do what we always do when we're confused. We eat.'

Lunching at Geoffrey's in Malibu, we sat outside, taking advantage of the majestic March weather. Though some parts of the city were apparently as hot as a tandoor, by the shore, it was exquisite.

Over baked brie and Chilean sea bass, Nitya pulled out her phone and called the only person she knew in the city – Manik Chouduri. A Delhi industrialist who had left his home to find fame and even more fortune in the City of Angels, he had been at college with her father. She arranged dinner at his house two nights later, told him she would be bringing a friend.

'Okay, so we're fed and happy,' she said, downing the last of her coffee. 'We need to have a plan. We're here for something. Let's make it happen.'

The next morning – I'd been awake since 4.30 a.m. – I Googled a company called Applied Automotives, one of the many I'd read about which was supposed to be part of the vanguard of developing cars that functioned purely on water.

'Oh, hello,' I said to the nasal-sounding receptionist who answered the phone. 'I'd like to come in and see, er,' I paused for a second, consulting the article I'd clipped, 'Mr Matthew Veitch.'

'Can I ask who's calling?'

'I'm from India,' I said, emphasizing the last word as if it were my cachet. 'I sent him an email last week?'

'Yes. But you are …?' she asked.

Clearly, being from India wasn't enough.

'Oh, my name is Sohana Badshah,' I said, asserting myself. 'I'm with Badshah Industries in Mumbai. We are looking for interesting investment opportunities. I'd like to set up a meeting with Mr Veitch.'

She put me on hold again. I spent a few minutes listening to Britney Spears.

'He's not in at the moment. But I'll make sure he gets your message,' the receptionist said, coming back.

There was no call-back from him, nor from anyone else I tried to contact, except the people at the biotech firm – that developed virtual cadavers for surgical residents – which had licensed the rights to its invention to a company in Pune.

'Let's see if my dad's friend can help,' said Nitya. I was grateful she was with me. I couldn't have handled all the rejection on my own.

Manik Chouduri lived in a house in Beverly Hills with a small swimming pool, an enormous dining room and a remote wife. He welcomed Nitya and me with a warm embrace. He wore a tweed cap on his bald head, insisted we visit the small shrine he had erected in a spare bedroom, and force-fed us pakodas and dhoklas.

'So, girls, what brings you here?' he asked.

Nitya gave him some details without revealing too much: my grandfather (of whom Manik Chouduri was aware) was actively seeking new opportunities, Los Angeles was a breeding ground for trailblazing ideas, and I had been dispatched to find some.

He looked sceptical, as if it were hardly a task to be entrusted to a young woman. He spooned more food onto our plates.

After dinner, he fed us Rocky Road ice-cream. Apart from the contents of his kitchen, he shared nothing. I felt disappointed; the evening had been a complete waste of time.

'I have an idea for you,' he said suddenly,

readjusting his cap as he chewed on a toothpick.
I turned towards Nitya, hopeful expectation in
my eyes.

'I'm developing a movie. We need financing.
If your family can provide that, maybe we can
talk.'

'What's the project?' I asked. I wasn't hopeful.
But maybe there was something there. Wild
profits had been realized from the most random
of ideas. One never knew.

'It's an animated film,' he said. 'Lots of CGI
and VFX. Could do great in the Indian market,
although I see potential in foreign territories
too. But we have to make it first. And that takes
money.'

'Uncle, I thought money wasn't a problem for
you,' said Nitya.

'Usually, it's not,' he said. 'But I still have to
get family approval on anything over a certain
amount. And they are not sure they want to fund
this. It is outside their comfort zone, as we say
here in America.'

'What's the movie about?' I asked.

He started talking and my brain dropped
out of the conversation in two minutes. Some
convoluted plot about robots, and set to
Bollywood music. I didn't know much about
movie ideas, but I knew that this one was

colossally bad. Especially attached to a $34 million price tag.

'Send me some literature,' I said, knowing that whatever written sales pitch he would courier to me would end up in the trash chute of Shutters.

'Well that was a pointless exercise,' I said to Nitya as we took a taxi back to our hotel. 'I was hoping he'd have some genius ideas for us, and instead he wants to milk my family.'

Nitya picked at a palmful of supari she had taken from the Chouduri home and glanced sideways at me.

'Get used to it,' she said.

On day four, upon returning to the hotel room after a brisk morning walk on the beach, a message lay waiting for me: Martin Veitch, the man who was developing hydrogen-powered cars for the mass market, had finally deigned to call me back.

'How can I help you?' he asked.

I spilled out the spiel I had prepared – how I was a representative from Badshah Industries in India which was looking at cutting-edge technology and new business opportunities, how I was in California to scout for new ideas, how I felt hydrogen-fuelled cars were the wave of the future – and asked if there was some way we could work together.

Feel free to Google us, I told him, and I could hear his fingers whiz along the keyboard as we spoke.

Five hours later, I was sitting in the office of Applied Automotives in a warehouse-like space in Culver City. Out in the courtyard was a prototype of a vehicle that ran on no gas, and which looked like any other auto out there were it not for the fact that a high-tech fuel cell gave it all its juice.

Martin Veitch came out to the lobby to meet me; he was African American, younger than I'd imagined, with a tattoo of Chinese characters down one arm, and dressed in distressed jeans and a hoodie. Had I not known him to be the CEO, I would have taken him for an office boy.

'Thanks for coming in,' he said, leading me to his office – basically a large cement box filled with more gadgets than I could count. Through the plate glass windows, I could see the rest of the staff, all dressed as casually as the boss, one whizzing down the corridor on sneakers that had wheels embedded in the soles. My grandfather would have a meltdown if his employees turned up to work like this.

Martin turned on a PowerPoint presentation, giving me reams and reams of facts about renewable energy, and scientific mumbo-jumbo about how hydrogen reacts with oxygen in a fuel cell to run electric motors. I desisted from mentioning to him that I had flunked chemistry at school.

More information followed. What the drawbacks and obstacles were (there were plenty, it appeared): storing, transporting and filling the liquid hydrogen in cars, the massive investments in infrastructure, and getting production processes up to snuff. He presented all these facts to me as if I were an equal, more an interested party than some heiress on vacation, and for that, I was grateful.

'Where is your company in terms of renewable energy projects?' he asked.

'It's something we are actively exploring,' I replied. It was the truth, after all: cold fusion, as I had discovered Sharan's pet project to be, was another cutting-edge, cheap and effective form of energy.

'Here's what's happening at our end,' said Martin. He swivelled his chair around to face me.

'We've had three offers from major automotive makers to buy us out. We're not going there. We don't want to be co-opted. A lot of people in the automotive industry don't want to see that happen. Look what became of the electric car. Our dream is to make hydrogen-powered transport a staple of the future, and there is no reason why that shouldn't happen.'

I admired his passion. I leaned forward in my seat.

'What do you need?' I asked, knowing the answer.

'Money, of course. Our funding is close to drying up. Venture capital firms were throwing millions at companies like us five years ago. Now, unless they see an immediate return, nobody is interested.'

He handed over an information kit and a hard copy of the presentation he had made.

'Take this back to your people,' he said. 'It lays out why this is a fantastic opportunity for anyone who wants to get in on a revolutionary new way of thinking about transportation. The world is going to be a very different place ten years from now. We need partners who share the vision.'

I stood up to leave, reached out my hand to shake his.

'Oh, do you have a business card?' he asked, almost as an afterthought.

That hadn't even occurred to me.

'I'm sorry, no. I forgot to bring one,' I lied. I'd

never had a business card. What would I have written on it?

'You know where I am,' he said, walking me out. 'Let's see if we can make something happen here.'

Back at Shutters, I told Nitya about the meeting and showed her the information pack.

'Put it in your back pocket,' she said.

'Huh?'

'Hang on to it, but keep looking. There are more options out there. We just have to find them.'

We had two more days in Los Angeles before we were scheduled to fly back to Mumbai. It felt like a rushed trip, but Nitya wanted to get back to her family. And while my time there had not been as rousing a success as I had hoped, at least I had *something*. At least I wouldn't be going back completely empty handed.

That evening, I settled down on the floor of our room to repack my suitcase. In the considerable time I'd had to myself on the so-called business trip, I had indulged in a fair bit of shopping. And with the jeggings I'd found at Kitson, the rhinestone-flecked tees at Lisa Kline, tunics from Tory Burch for my mother and vintage comics for Milan, I realized I might need to purchase another suitcase.

I began carefully putting my new purchases into my big black case with the red handles, the one that accompanied me on every trip. When it looked like I was running out of space, I flipped it around. On the underside was a zippered compartment, hidden from view. If I could ascertain how much I could cram in there, I could perhaps go out and shop some more. I slid my hand inside. My fingers closed around a rustling plastic bag which I fished out. The first thing I saw was a light blue sweater, one sleeve crossed on top, a small piece of yarn unravelled from its wrist. I remembered the night I had gently pulled at it.

Jag's stuff. What he had left behind on the day he had walked out on me. I had shoved it into my suitcase at the last minute when leaving the apartment in London, too disconsolate to consider the pointlessness of carrying the clothing of a man who wished to never see me again.

Back in Mumbai, Chanoo had unpacked my stuff and had clearly neglected the zipper.

Now I pulled out the sweater, held it to my face, like they do in movies where a parent has lost a child. It still carried his scent. After all that time, I was as vulnerable. I felt a jab in the pit of my stomach, a longing for him.

I finished packing but left Jag's things on top of the dresser. Later, I told Nitya what they were.

She stared at me, her face thoughtful. Then she stood up from the edge of the bed where she had been sitting, crossed the room and went to my computer.

'Yup, he's still there,' she said as she angled the screen towards me. It was his company's website. There he was, under 'Our Team'. A brief bio, a thumbnail image of him in a suit and no tie, a casual corporate shot.

Nitya and I stared at each other. She raised her eyebrows, as if asking me a question she could not say out loud, then slammed the laptop shut.

Early the next morning, we checked out of our room. Thirty minutes later, Nitya was behind the wheel of a rented Honda, me in the seat next to hers. Between us lay a printout of directions to our hotel in San Francisco. On another page was a map of an area east of Union Square, where Jag's office was located.

We sped up Pacific Coast Highway. Five hundred-some miles to where Jag was. We had no idea if he was even going to be there.

'This is a bad idea, Nitya,' I said. 'You can't just drop in on someone like that.'

'You have to do this, Sohana,' she said. 'If you get on that plane tomorrow night without even trying to see him, you'll regret it. Trust me. It doesn't matter what happens now. All that matters is that you give it a shot.'

She turned the car radio on, and Katy Perry began singing about teenage dreams. It was a stunning day, the kind of breathtakingly bright morning you saw in postcards from Los Angeles. It felt almost unreal. Nitya slipped on her sunglasses, relaxed back in her seat, pressed her foot on the accelerator, and drove.

TWENTY-THREE

At ten the next morning, Nitya and I took a taxi from the Mandarin Oriental in San Francisco to Jag's office. I was holding his bag of clothes. A look of concerned encouragement on her face, she pushed me towards the lobby as if it were my first day at school, then said she would meet me in the Starbucks next door.

'What if he's not in?' I asked her, feeling nauseous with nerves.

'Then find out when he'll be back.'

'What if he throws me out? What if he refuses to see me? What if …' My voice trailed off. A million scenarios played through my head, each ridiculous, each real. What if he was bonking a woman in his office? What if he was dead?

'Look at it like this,' Nitya said, now leading me towards the bank of elevators. 'No matter what happens today, one thing is for sure: by the time you leave this place, you will know more than you did when you came. You will have clarity. You will have closure.'

I hated that word, the clichéd finality of it. I knew there was rarely such a thing. But I got Nitya's point, and couldn't argue that it was a valid one.

The lift opened on the fifth floor. A big sign in front of me read 'GoGreenNRG', with burnished gold lettering on a forest-green background. I walked through a huge glass door on my right. A receptionist sat behind a desk, wearing a headset, her eyes fixed on a computer screen. She looked up when I walked in.

'Yes, can I help you?' she asked brightly.

'I'm here to see Jag … um, Jagdish? – Sachdev,' I said. I was trembling. I was glad I had been too nervous to eat breakfast, or I would have thrown it all up.

The receptionist punched something into her keyboard, looked at a calendar that popped up on her screen.

'Was he expecting you?' she asked. 'I don't see anything scheduled.'

'I'm a friend,' I said. 'I came into town at the last minute. Just thought I'd drop by and see if he was here. But it doesn't matter. It's not important.'

I was relieved. I could leave the place, go back to Nitya, have an espresso and a blueberry muffin. I could tell her I had tried.

The door behind me opened.

'Sohana?'

I'd recognize that voice anywhere. Decades could pass and that voice wouldn't fade from my memory.

I turned around. Jag was standing right in front of me. He had a flat leather messenger bag on his shoulder, heavy, I could tell, by the way the strap dragged his shirt so his collar was askew. He looked like he had just seen a ghost.

'What are you doing here?' he asked. Then, remembering the presence of the receptionist, he forced a smile. He wasn't the sort to allow even a whiff of drama to enter his workplace.

'I was visiting San Francisco,' I said. I was breathing heavily, like an asthmatic. 'With Nitya.' I had told him plenty about her during those long, intimate chats in London. Saying her name now took me back to that zone, creating an ephemeral bridge to a time I had hoped by now to forget.

'I remembered where you worked,' I said, as if knowing his place of business was the only thing that justified my being there.

The parcel of clothes was in my now-sweaty hands. 'You forgot this,' I said, holding it out. 'When you left.'

It was as if the world around us had gone mute. The receptionist caught a glimpse of my face and quickly looked away.

'Come with me,' he said. He led the way down a busy, brightly lit hallway. His office had his name on the door, underneath it the words 'Vice President, Origination and Trading'. We went inside and he shut the door. Thankfully, there were no glass walls there. I was self-conscious enough.

'I can't believe you're here,' he said.

I couldn't tell if he meant that in a good way or not. He motioned to a chair, asked me to sit. He dropped his bag onto the floor, and instead of going to the opposite side of his desk, he pulled a chair next to mine. He leaned forward so his elbows touched his knees, his arms crossed in front of him. It was a classic Jag stance – one that indicated compassion, connection, attentiveness. I wasn't sure if he was feeling any of those things, but took comfort from the fact that he was at ease enough to lapse into that position.

'What's going on?' he asked. His eyes were filled with concern.

I loved and hated him for it. In a way, he was acting as if nothing had ever soured between us. As if I had just seen him the day before. But it was also infuriatingly patronizing, like I was someone who needed to be talked down from jumping off a ledge.

'Everything's fine,' I said, contriving to get some

cheer into my voice. 'I've had your clothes for all this time. The maid left them in my suitcase, from London. I didn't even see them till we were in LA last week. I was there to check out some business opportunities for my family.' I liked saying that last part, as if it would elevate me in his eyes, make me more interesting, more worthy. But, above all, I wanted to be casual, carefree. This was some great coincidence, and I was here for nothing more than to return his stuff. I wasn't heartbroken at all.

'Oh, and you know what? I learned how to cook,' I said. 'I took lessons. I even threw a dinner party. I made everything myself.' I was babbling now.

Jag took the bag of clothes from me and flung it on a couch behind him.

'That's great,' he said. 'But I don't want to talk about cooking right now. Tell me how *you* are.'

Anger surged through me. The smile on my face now felt stilted, frozen.

'How do you think I am?' I asked.

He took a deep breath, straightened himself. It seemed as if he was about to say something appeasing, calming, but he was too late. The channels had been opened. I had nothing to lose.

'You walked out on me,' I said. 'Despite everything we had together, you just left. You didn't even give me a chance to make things right.'

'I felt like shit,' he said. 'After that last time we spoke, I wanted to call you a hundred more times.'

'Then why didn't you?'

'I flew to New Jersey to see my dad,' he said. 'I wanted to understand everything, have him tell me that it was all a mistake. But, man, that wasn't happening. Your uncle really did a number on him.'

'And how do you know that it's your father who has been wronged?' I asked. My arms were crossed defensively in front of me. Maybe Manjuli's information was inaccurate. Maybe it was *his* father who had been the swindler and my uncle the one who was swindled.

Jag sighed.

'I looked at the paperwork,' he said. 'I know the facts and don't want to get into it now because it's not productive. But my father trusted your uncle and he ended up getting screwed.'

'Well, isn't it over now, anyway?' I said. 'I read that a court ruled in your dad's favour.'

'He hasn't seen a dime,' Jag said. 'Your uncle is appealing. He's just going to drag this thing out.' He shook his head, visibly frustrated.

'I am *not* my uncle,' I said. 'Whatever happened

between your dad and Amit Badshah has nothing to do with me. With *us*. Why couldn't you just tell him that?'

Jag stood up, walked to the window, looked out over the city. I could see the reflection of his face in the glass.

'You know as well as I do that it's not so easy. There's no way I can marry a girl whose uncle has caused so much damage to my family.'

I wasn't going to sit there and beg him to love me again. I couldn't even insist that Jag was wrong, because he wasn't. Where I came from, wrongs committed – especially in business – lasted an awfully long time.

'I'm going to go now,' I said, standing up. 'I don't know what I was thinking by coming here. It was Nitya's idea. I guess she thought it would settle things in my mind.' I picked up my handbag.

'I'm so sorry, Sohana,' he said. 'I never meant for you to get hurt. I hate how things turned out.'

I opened the door and left. I walked down the hallway alone, holding my breath, knowing that if I allowed myself even a second to exhale, I'd start crying like a baby. I had to make it out of there, into the elevator, back to Nitya.

Not for the first time, I just wanted to go home.

We decided to change our tickets so that we could fly back to Mumbai from San Francisco the next day. Nitya tiptoed around me like I was a widow in mourning. I wasn't quite sure what she had expected the outcome of my meeting with Jag to be. That he would give me a mixed tape? An engagement ring? A smooch in the closet?

When it became evident from the way I walked into Starbucks that there was no such happy ending, she looked guilty, as if the freshness of my wounds was all her fault. It was. Whatever progress I had made in trying to forget Jag over the past few months had been set back in the worst way. It was like he had dumped me all over again.

I was on the phone in our hotel room with the airline, figuring out schedules and surcharges, when my iPhone buzzed on the bed. It was a text, from Jag. Two words: 'Drinks 2nite?'

My first impulse was to text him back asking him to bugger off, to tell him that I hated him. Nitya grabbed the phone from me before my fingers could do any damage.

'Hear him out,' she said, aware of the irony of her request. '*He's* coming to you this time. It's different. Go see what he has to say.'

I texted him back. 'MO Bar. Six p.m.'

He was already there when I arrived. He stood

up when I walked in, kissed me on the cheek as if he were an old acquaintance and hadn't just devastated me. Live piano music, soft lighting, quiet conversation around us – it was a scene set for romance, but I knew better than to expect any of that now.

He asked me if I was hungry. We ordered sushi and fried shishito peppers, which he said were his favourite things there. I wondered whom he used to come with. I wanted something exotic to drink, something adventurous, and asked the waiter to bring me a lychini. He went for an Amstel Light, practical to a fault.

'So?' I said, the chore of ordering dealt with. 'What do you want?'

I was being insufferably rude and knew it. I was still bristling with hurt from our exchange that morning but wanted to come off as heroic, unfeeling. It was an exercise in pointlessness. Jag always managed to see through me.

'I wanted to see you again,' he said. 'I felt bad about how we left things this morning. I just wanted you to know that it was never about you. I really loved you, and leaving you was the hardest thing I've ever had to do. But when family is involved, everything becomes complicated. You should know that better than anyone.'

My defences crumbled. I could never fault Jag

for his sincerity, for his ability to speak the truth, even if I hated hearing it.

Our drinks arrived. I took a big sip, felt the warmth of the alcohol sweep through my body. The vodka hit my head almost instantly, giving me a nice, clean buzz. Milan was right.

'Tell me again what you're doing in the States,' he said.

I told him everything. The newspaper article. My grandfather's decree. The freezing out of the three brothers. The frenzy that had descended on the grandsons. My alliance with Milan. The decision to go to LA. My folder of clippings. The disappointment that was Manik Chouduri. The potential that was Martin Veitch. I talked to him as easily, as freely, as I had always done.

'You're on the right track,' he said. 'I mean, your instincts are spot on. The things that you're looking at – those are going to be the industries of the future.'

'I'm flying home tomorrow,' I said. 'I want to be able to go back to Milan with something firm. He's counting on me.'

Jag bent down to get his bag. From it, he pulled out a clear plastic folder, which he handed over to me.

'What's this?' I asked, peering through the low lighting.

'Something brand new. Just developed at a major university here. This is what the world needs. It's what *India* needs, what you should take back to your cousin.'

I skimmed the top page. It was a brief about a miniscule solar cell – based on the principles of photosynthesis – that could use sunlight and water to power an entire house.

'It's not that different from what your hydrogen-powered car guy might have talked to you about,' he said. 'The concept is the same, but this is much more tangible, much more accessible. It's a tiny gizmo, the size of a credit card. It's cheap to make. You don't need that much to get it up and running. And it can deliver an affordable basic power system. Once news of it gets out, everyone will want it. But you have to be the first to take it back. Get in touch with the developers. See how you can acquire the rights to it.'

Something about the information felt right, valid. More than that, I trusted the source. Jag was nothing if not astute. If he vouched for something, it had to be worthwhile.

'Why are you doing this?' I asked. 'Why are you helping me?'

'Come on, Sohana,' he said a little impatiently. 'No matter why things didn't work out between us, I was really in love with you.' Was. The operative word. 'You deserved better. I feel like, in some small way, I should try and make it up to you.'

I appreciated all that was coming from him and the motivation behind it, but it wasn't what I wanted to hear. I didn't want some scrambling recompense for an old hurt. I just wanted him to love me again.

I shoved a piece of sushi into my mouth, downed the rest of my drink.

'I'd better go,' I said. 'I have to finish packing before we leave.'

'I have a question for you,' Jag said as he motioned to our waiter for the bill.

'What?'

'Why not you?'

'Why not me what?'

'Why not *you* as a candidate to take over the family business? Why does it have to be one of the boys? You are here. Not Milan. You found the information. He didn't. So why not you?'

'Don't be ridiculous, Jag,' I said. 'I don't know anything about running a business. One of the boys will get it. That much has been decided.'

'I think,' said Jag, scribbling his signature on the credit card slip, 'that you know more than you give yourself credit for. Don't underestimate yourself, Sohana Badshah. I know the kind of woman you are.'

I stood up, held the folder he had given me to my chest. 'Yes,' I said crisply, 'but you left me anyway.'

I turned and walked away from him.

As I waited for the lift, he showed up next to me. The elevator doors opened. He stepped in alongside me. I reached out, pressed my floor number. He pushed the button for the lobby. There were just the two of us. He reached over and took my hand. I let him. He caressed my fingers. The doors opened at my floor. He pulled me to him, kissed me fully.

'I've never stopped thinking about you,' he whispered into my ear.

I pulled back. 'No good can come of this,' I said quietly. 'I'm going home tomorrow. You've made your choice.'

I got out, and didn't wait for the doors to shut behind me.

TWENTY-FOUR

Once I returned home, Milan dropped by unexpectedly to take me out for a post-dinner drink at Indigo Deli.

'Chachi, she's jetlagged,' Milan implored my mother who was stridently against me going out. I had had dinner, brushed my teeth, and was planning on a dose of melatonin and an early night when Milan had come visiting. But, in my mother's far more sensible view of the world, once a girl was in her pyjamas for the night, she stayed in them.

'Milan, she has just flown back. Let the girl rest.'

Milan turned towards me, a beseeching look in his eyes. I knew my cousin well enough to know when he needed me for something, even just to hang out.

'Ma, I'll go just for a short while,' I said. 'I'll order chamomile tea there. It will help me sleep.'

'Chanoo can make you chamomile tea here,'

she said. She was annoyed at her nephew for provoking me that way, rousing me from what had been a relaxed, if sleepless, evening in.

'Seriously, Mom. Just an hour. Please?'

Milan grinned his cheeky smile. Even my mother was not immune to the boy's many charms.

At Indigo, we grabbed a booth. I had brought along the information from Martin Veitch, as well as what Jag had given me. We leaned close to each other beneath the swinging copper lamp as if the place were replete with corporate spies.

I told him about Manik Chouduri, the ridiculous movie idea, his request for $34 million.

'But forget about all that. Here's what I think you should be looking at,' I said, pushing the folders across the table to him.

He glanced at the paperwork about the photosynthesis microchip. Jag's business card was tucked in the back. I had forgotten to remove it.

'So you saw the man, did you?' he asked. 'Figured you would. Didn't think you'd go all the way to California without looking in on him.'

'I didn't plan to,' I said. 'It was Nitya's idea.'

'Sure it was.' He paused. 'How did it go? Will we finally be getting rid of you, once and for all?'

'Please,' I said as I pulled my shawl around me, shielding myself from a blast of air-conditioning whooshing out of an overhead vent. 'He's a fool.'

'And you, clearly, are still in love with him,' said Milan.

We were interrupted at our table by Anushka who stood in all her glory, wearing a striking sunflower yellow dress that clung to her every flab-free curve.

'Hi,' I said. I had not been expecting her. I may as well still have been in my pyjamas, that's how dowdy I felt in her presence.

'Sohana, darling, so great to see you again!' she trilled. She leaned down, gave me a kiss. Her fragrance was fresh. She slid into the seat next to my cousin.

'Great you could make it,' Milan said, reaching out and touching Anushka's hand.

So this was what had transpired since I'd been away: a love affair between my constantly randy cousin and an improbably hot actress. He was beguiled by her and smiled as she slipped her hand onto his leg. I sighed. She would be another one of Milan's flings, destined to be cast off when he got bored. I had had lunches that were longer than Milan's relationships.

'How was your trip, Soh?' she said, calling me by the name that Milan did.

'Very good, actually,' I said. 'I'm hoping to turn my cousin here into a captain of industry.'

The restaurant door opened and we saw Pawan standing in the entranceway, glancing around.

The evening was full of surprises. I wondered who might show up next. Now it looked as if Pawan might be looking for someone else. But his eyes landed on our trio and he made his way towards us.

'Hi,' I said. 'What are you doing here?'

I became aware of how thoughtless the remark was as soon as it left my mouth.

'I called on your house to speak with you,' he said. 'Chachi told me you were here. With him.' He motioned with his head to Milan, and then began staring at Anushka blankly. She smiled at him, a little guiltily I thought, and then quickly looked away.

'Hey, Bro,' said Milan. 'Join us.'

I moved in so he could sit next to me. There was something strange about him that night, a wildness in his eyes I'd never seen before. If I didn't know him better, I'd think he was high.

Pawan ordered a tiny tumbler of Jose Cuervo, straight. It was sweet, golden and, as I knew it to be, a panacea for the wretched. He downed it in one gulp and slammed the glass on the table like a lone alcoholic at a bar in a B-movie. His eyes glazed over.

He was wearing a striped blue-and-white, short-sleeved shirt, like a mid-level executive. He looked incongruous in the graffiti-teed and silk-shirted crowd. His eyes fell on the folders on the table. Milan picked them up, moved them away.

Pawan turned towards me.

'Looks like you had a productive trip,' he said.

Like the rest of the family, Pawan had been told that I had gone on a shopping-and-sightseeing trip to Los Angeles with my best friend. But somewhere down the line, he'd figured out the truth. Now I felt compelled to reach out, put my hand on his arm. He seemed so alone.

'You two an item?' he asked Milan and Anushka. Pawan had ogled her at my house. Seeing his brother with her must have crushed him.

'We're just friends,' lied Anushka.

'How special,' said Pawan bitterly. 'Friends.'

More drinks appeared, some food. Pawan ploughed into a platter of home fries doused with ketchup, licking the tangy red sauce off his fingers.

An uneasy silence fell on the table. I tried to lessen the awkwardness by chattering inconsequentially about LA's glorious weather and the tours of stars' homes that Nitya and I had taken just for the fun of it. We had seen mansions shielded by wrought-iron gates, and Nitya was convinced that she had spotted Charlie Sheen as we had cruised down Rodeo Drive.

'I love Charlie Sheen,' Milan said. 'He's a kindred spirit.'

'What? You mean the whole bad boy thing?' Anushka asked. Her chin was cupped in her hand and she was pressed right up next to him.

'He doesn't apologize for who he is,' Milan said. 'I think that's awesome.'

Pawan was listening stoically, silently. I knew drunk well enough to know he was already there. Then, without saying a word, he got up from the table and walked over to the other side of the eatery.

The place was famous for, among other things, its extensive wine supply; bottles were slotted into grooves stacked up to the ceiling and a movable ladder slid along the length of the walls.

Pawan stood by the ladder, clutching one of its rungs, staring at the three of us. Before I knew what was happening, he began to climb up.

'Shit,' said Milan. He pushed Anushka out of her seat and sprinted over to where his twin had been standing just seconds ago.

'Come down, Pawan,' he said, shouting. 'Come on. Stop acting like an idiot.'

Pawan was on the uppermost rung now, staring down. Seconds earlier, the entire room had been filled with chatter. Now, it was so quiet, I could hear the hiss of a boiling pot in the kitchen. A restaurant manager rushed to the bottom of the ladder.

'Sir, please, I request you to climb down,' he said politely, his face turned upwards.

If it was America, a SWAT team would be there already.

'Whatever it is you need, sir, we can help you. But please, you first come down.'

I stopped breathing. A real-life drama was unspooling in front of me – my own cousin was unravelling – and I had no idea what to do. So I stayed where I was, uselessly.

Pawan remained at the top of the ladder. Everyone, me included, waited to see what he would do next, how soon it would take him to realize his madness and begin his descent into contrition.

But Pawan clung to the rungs and turned around until he was facing the rows of dark glass bottles. He pulled one out, stared at its label, held it for a second in a trembling hand, then let it fall.

The manager jumped to the side just before the bottle crashed, leaving a dark pool of Bordeaux on the floor. A collective gasp in the room, eyes still fixed upwards, hands all around on mouths. Pawan yanked another bottle out, dropped it. He let it fall straight down. It crashed inches away from the first. Then he threw a third.

Milan began ascending the ladder, scrambling up behind his brother. A few rungs below, he reached up, held his twin's ankle.

'Please, Pawan,' he said. It was the first time I'd ever seen Milan supplicant to his brother, lower down than him. 'Please, stop. I'm so sorry for everything.' His voice was filled with deference.

Pawan glanced at his twin, half-considering his request, his apology. From where I was sitting, I couldn't see his eyes, just his spectacle lenses, reflecting the lights in the room. I couldn't see my cousin's pain. I thought that if I could, I might have been able to help him, but then realized I'd seen it all along, but had done nothing. None of us had.

Pawan pulled out another bottle. He held it aloft, steadily. He looked downwards at his brother. Then, as all eyes were fixed on the two boys, Pawan gingerly put the bottle back in its slot. Milan exhaled. Pawan began inching down the ladder, spurring Milan downwards.

Milan waited at the bottom for his brother. They stood there, staring at each other. Milan's underarms were patchy with sweat. The room was still silent, save for some employees who had appeared to sweep up the mess. Milan and Pawan walked back to the table and sat down.

Pawan resumed eating his fries.

'Did you see any other famous people in LA?' Milan asked.

I was still too stunned to speak and shook my head.

'Next time, then,' he said.

Chatter filled the room again. It was as if nothing had gone amiss. This was Mumbai at its finest – heart-wrenching drama, twisted and scandalous, but it didn't matter. We were inured to it. We just rolled on.

When it was time to leave, the manager came by with the bill and handed it to Milan: in addition to the food and drink we had consumed were listed three bottles of wine. Pawan, in his inebriated, disconsolate state, had happened to choose some of the priciest ones on the menu to fling down to the floor.

Milan didn't give the bill a second glance. He fished out his credit card, slapped it down on the small black plastic tray and handed it over to the manager. He looked at his brother, a hint of sorrow in his eyes.

'Are you cool?' Milan asked Pawan.

'Yes,' came the reply.

TWENTY-FIVE

By April, there were only three letters of the alphabet on everyone's lips: NCL. The National Cricket League. At dinner parties and art gallery openings, on the rarefied green lawns of the Willingdon Club and side-by-side under the hot gush of hair drying stations at the city's salons, the topic of conversation gravitated towards this mother lode of national sport. And the topics ranged from the insightful to the banal: who was the best-looking player on the field, did the Kolkata team stand a chance, and was there a spot on a friend's helicopter to the match in Mohali?

All the men in my family wished they had dreamed up this fantastically money making and gloriously satisfying franchise. Sharan often talked about how much fun, how *impressive* it would be to own a team.

'Finals,' Milan said, holding up a couple of small black boxes. 'Chennai versus Delhi. It's huge.' Inside were glossy tags affixed to neck cords, which were our tickets to the event at a massive stadium in Navi Mumbai.

I looked at him wearily. I had never had a grand passion for the game, and that night, I wanted to stay home.

'I'm just not feeling very social these days, Milan,' I said.

'Come on!' he said. 'No self-respecting Mumbai society girl turns this stuff down. It'll be awesome! A bunch of us are going. The whole Badshah clan.' He pulled my ticket out of its box and threw it around my head like a garland.

'There,' he said. 'You're coming.'

We all carpooled from Malini's house. I ended up going with Milan and Pawan and their mother and mine, the rest of our extended clan following in a series of dark Mercedes Benzes, like some mafia convoy. Milan wondered aloud why we weren't in a helicopter, like most of his friends. His mother pointed out that it was because Baba didn't own one, and most likely never would.

'Wait till I'm boss,' Milan whispered into my ear.

The twins were squashed next to each other in the rear seat of the car, sharing the headset to Pawan's iPod, each using one ear bud. He had downloaded a business management audio book and they would occasionally stop listening, turn to each other and have a conversation, like equals.

Our driver was silent with envy as he drove us to the venue. We were dropped off at the end of a long, gravelly road and shown into the VIP enclosure where cricket buffs far more ardent than I will ever be gazed through big, smudged glass windows at the bright green turf, around which throngs of tiny faceless people were packed.

The other Badshahs joined us. Malini was in a fire-engine red, figure-hugging dress with a thick gold belt at her waist, with matching red talons and high-heeled white shoes. She was so loud and joyous at joining us at our table, one would've thought she hadn't seen us a couple of hours earlier but a few decades ago. She was in an especially good mood. Karan held a glass of whisky; he and Armaan were telling each other salty jokes. My father directed me to the heaving buffet table, pointing out the authentic Sindhi dishes – pakwan, papad and pickles.

'Why don't you obsess about one of the players?' Milan said, noticing the bored look on my face. 'All the girls have their favourites.' He pointed towards someone in an electric blue jersey from the Delhi team, the red lettering declaring his last name.

Even I had heard of Vivek Abbas. Now his hair shone golden in the floodlights, a cascade of chocolate-hued curls, small silver loops in his ears, his signature. He was, despite my jaundiced view of both boys and sports, and even from that distance, absolutely gorgeous with his pants curved around a near-perfect behind and his stomach rigid beneath his shirt. I turned towards one of the TVs. The cameras zoomed in on him. He wore an expression of calm intensity and stood with his head tilted as he listened to a teammate.

'After the way he's been playing this season, he's sure to be picked for the national team,' Milan said. 'You like?'

I smiled, shrugged my shoulders.

'Listen, there's an after-party. Let me make some calls. We'll go.' He pulled out his phone.

I put my hand on his. 'Thanks, Milan. He's very cute. But I'm really not interested right now.'

Armaan was standing alone, leaning against the glass. I went to him. Though we technically lived under the same roof, sometimes days passed without me seeing him.

'Hi, Sis,' he said. 'Try?' He handed over a glass of something orange. I took a sip. It was fruity but deadened with some kind of alcohol.

At that moment, I just liked the fact that I was

standing next to him. He was my big brother, my real brother. He would always be there for me, blessing me at the wedding I hoped to have one day, laying his hand on mine as I was about to be joined with another.

But, still, I felt far removed from him. He knew nothing about Jag, or the real reason behind my trip to LA. I had always kept secrets from him, as if he were some disapproving parent. Now, positioned next to him, I wanted to tell him everything.

'I'm sorry,' I said. I was holding a plate of biryani, tiny green peas and black cloves mushed into grains of white rice.

'For what?'

'Oh, just stuff,' I said.

He looked at me, and in that moment I knew that he knew; that even though he and I had the same parents, Milan had always been more of a brother to me. That if Milan and Armaan were caught in a raging river, and if I could only choose one to save, I could not, right then, without a shadow of a doubt, say whom I would reach for. That fact suddenly saddened me.

'Have a drink,' he said. 'The bloody Marys are good.'

'How are things with Ekta?' I asked.

'Very good,' he said, his face spreading into a

warm smile. 'You know, I'm pretty sure that she is the one.'

'What?' I asked. 'Really?'

'Really,' he said, thoughtfully.

We turned towards the window to watch the game. My mind was still churning over Armaan's words. I had never seen him so serious about a woman. Baba might have a hard time with it; in his view of things, supermodels couldn't possibly make the best bahus. But I knew my brother, how determined he was. If he wanted to marry Ekta, he would.

But I couldn't stay distracted for long. Things on the greens were heating up and everyone was fixated.

The Chennai bowler was one of those left-handed wizards with a fearful reputation, intimidating batsmen with his legendary googly spins and a history of having taken over 800 wickets in his career. At the semi-finals, he had sliced his way through the team's batting line-up like a knife through warm butter.

Vivek Abbas went up, breezily chewing gum, settled into a protective stance and walloped the ball so hard, it went outside the pavilion. He scored a six right off the bat. It was a good omen. He batted the next three balls sedately and met the fourth attack with a resounding crack that sent the ball sailing over the heads of the outfielders. He raced back and forth and got in four runs before the ball was back in the game.

The bowler continued his attack with unwavering force.

Vivek either blocked the balls with impeccable timing or methodically rocketed them into the floodlit skies. Over after over, he churned out multiple runs, not to mention the seven sixes he got in before the end of the game. By the time the teams packed it in, he had clubbed out nearly 120 runs, single-handedly carrying his team to victory.

'Shit!' exclaimed Armaan excitedly. 'What the hell! What a game!'

Around the greens and up in the VIP enclosure, the fans were delirious. Even I could no longer be half-hearted. Watching Vivek take command of the game like that was unexpectedly thrilling. It had been magical, a show of athletic prowess. I felt fortunate to have been there to watch it unfold. Now, he was more attractive than ever. I reconsidered Milan's invitation to hit the after-parties.

After, chaos reigned outside the entrance. The men went off to find our cars and drivers, and Malini to use the restroom, leaving me with my mother and Preeti. The place was overrun with security guards, thin men in grimy green uniforms, carrying rifles. Coaches waited in the rear to ferry the teams away.

Vivek emerged, suitably jubilant, white towel coiled around his neck, surrounded by cheering teammates. He carried himself with the grace of a newly minted cricket star. On the back of his astonishing knock, he would no doubt land a bevy of lucrative endorsement deals.

I peered at him through the crowds as he reached into his bag for his phone and sent a text. Then he was gone from the melee.

I stood on tiptoe and craned my neck to follow him; his performance was electrifying and I was developing a smidgen of a crush on him. I spotted him half-hidden in the shadows. There was someone with him, someone with a flash of gold at her waist, towering on heels that made her almost as tall as him. I gasped. *Malini?*

Why would a woman in her mid-fifties, who had never displayed any real affinity towards cricket or its players, be engaged in a private conversation with the night's biggest star? She had never even mentioned that she knew Vivek. Now, they were talking with an easy familiarity. I turned to see if my mother or Preeti had noticed, but they were looking in the other direction, watching out for our car. I reverted my gaze towards Vivek and Malini. She reached out and, for just a flicker of a second, put her hand on his chest, her scarlet-tipped fingers disappearing inside the open buttons of his shirt so she was touching his skin.

If I had blinked, I would have missed it.

A minute later, Malini was back in our midst, a pink fluster in her cheeks.

'So glad I relieved myself before that long drive home,' she trilled.

I stared at her, grateful that I appeared to have been the only person to have noticed an intimate moment between my aunt and a dashing cricket player. The last thing my family needed was more drama.

TWENTY-SIX

'So you think they're doing the nasty?' Milan chuckled. I had called him as soon as I'd got home from the stadium to recount what I had seen transpiring between Malini and Vivek.

'I think there's *something* going on,' I said.

'Well, in that case, my high opinion of him has now officially been flushed down the toilet,' my cousin said. 'He might be the hottest cricket star of the season, but he's got crappy taste.'

'But ... do you think she would, Milan? You know, have an affair?' I couldn't even get the words out. Malini might be crass, overbearing, socially ambitious – but I couldn't imagine her sleeping with someone else. She had always put her family first. Not to mention that Vivek Abbas was young enough to be her son; he couldn't have been older than twenty-eight ... that would make him younger than Sharan and Karan. My skin crawled at the thought.

'People do surprising things sometimes,' said Milan. 'Just when you think you know someone, they turn around and do something out of character.'

In between obsessing over cricket scores for weeks and impressing Anushka, Milan had been busy trying to make things happen on the work front. Almost as if to justify my trip to Los Angeles, he regularly gave me progress reports: he had been in touch with Martin Veitch about the hydrogen-powered car, had contacted the university lab on the East Coast about the solar chip. He had even emailed Manik Chouduri about his film financing proposal. Milan told me he wanted to explore everything, leave no stone unturned.

'I've had second thoughts about what I asked you to do,' he said to me one evening as we chatted quietly in a corner at Baba's house.

'What, the spying stuff?' I said, beginning to feel relieved.

'Back off when it comes to Pawan,' he said. 'He's my brother.'

'Well, shabaash to you for figuring that out,' I said.

'I still want to beat Sharan and Karan. In the end, if it's down to Pawan and me, so be it. May the best man win.'

A week later, Manjuli Khosla called me.

'I'm checking in,' she said. 'You said you'd give me the scoop. I'm still waiting.'

'Nothing has been decided yet,' I told her. 'I need a little more time.'

'My editor is really pushing me. The rumours around town are heating up. I'm going to have to deliver something to him soon.'

'A few weeks, please, Manjuli, okay?'

It served as a wake-up call. I had to move quickly.

'Hey, Karan, how's it going?' I asked.

I had sidled up to him at an orphanage in Byculla that Dadi was an inveterate supporter of. Every few months, Dadi enlisted the help of any available family members to go there and hand out to the children fully stocked Sponge Bob pencil cases, Spiderman backpacks and flashing green yo-yos. Given that her excursions were often in the middle of work days, most of the cousins had a good enough reason not to tag along. But I was almost always there, happy for the chance to venture out and spend time with my grandmother. That day, Karan had joined us, having come over after a meeting not far away, and brandishing a bag of colourful T-shirts which were shipping samples from a factory he worked with in Karachi.

'Everything is good,' he said, watching from the sidelines as the director of the orphanage made the thin, small children stand up and pay their respects to Dadi who was seated formally on a low stage. 'I just really need to get out of here,' he said, glancing at his watch. 'I have a meeting back at the office at three.'

'Anybody interesting?' I asked, a little guiltily. I would make a pathetic covert agent.

'Just a banker,' he said as he handed over the bag of T-shirts to a staff member who was stacking them on a table in order of size.

'Oh,' I said, pointlessly.

There had to be a way for me to get more out of him. Karan's phone rang and he reached for it. An orphanage staffer asked me if I thought the tangerine coloured shirts could be worn by boys as well as girls. As I considered her question, I had half an ear trained on what my cousin was saying.

'Yes,' he hissed, irritated, into the phone. 'Kamal Patel from United Bank is coming over later. I told you already. He'll give us the financing. Please, stop worrying. I'll call you when I have something.' He hung up quickly, stuck his phone back into the front pocket of his jacket and looked even more exasperated now.

The ceremony with Dadi was taking forever. The children were being led in a song, a stilted, formal piece that had been written for the occasion, in honour of my grandmother. A little girl, younger than Rajan, went on stage to hand Dadi a floppy bouquet of flowers. The director was speaking into a microphone now, talking about how the generous donations from Rukmani Badshah had helped keep the place going and helped fund the construction of a new clinic on the grounds. Dadi smiled benevolently, her beige chiffon sari and South Sea pearl necklace shimmering under a couple of spotlights. She was every inch the elegant matriarch and philanthropist. She was also wilful and strong-headed; anybody else would have been astonished that she and Baba had been harmoniously married all these years, given his gruffness and her recalcitrance. But I understood Dadi. She would often say to me that she and I were the same person, two generations apart. When it came to Baba, she always knew when to give in, just so, just to keep the peace, a steely knowing in her eyes. She knew how to let him think he was the boss. Of all the things that Dadi knew – and she knew a lot – she knew best how to be a wife.

'Excuse me, miss,' Karan now asked of a passing staff member. 'Where's the restroom?' The room was stiflingly hot and he wiped beads of sweat off his forehead with a handkerchief.

The woman pointed the way. Karan was about to trot off when he stopped, turned around, took off his jacket and threw it over the back of a chair.

'Watch that, okay?' he said, pointing to it.

I can't believe what I did next. I made sure Karan was safely out of the picture, and then reached into his pocket and pulled out his phone. It was horrible. Beyond subtly foraging for information. I was snooping now. In most circumstances, this was a punishable offence.

I scrolled through Karan's recent calls; the one he had just taken was from someone whose caller ID had come up as R. Dutta. Could that be Ravi Dutta, son of the major industrialist Chandru Dutta? I knew Karan and Ravi were friends – rich boys, after all, tended to hang out with other rich boys. But why would Ravi call, and what did he have to do with whatever financing Karan was trying to arrange? Could this be linked to Karan's purported bid for the family business? I didn't even know the right questions to ask. Instead, I did what I always did – thought of Milan. I grabbed a piece of paper lying on a table. On the front was a drawing by one of the girls – she had scrawled her name, Jayanti, at the bottom, in yellow crayon. It was of her with a couple standing outside a red-roofed house, holding a ball. Stick drawings of a mother, a father and a basket of fruit on a picnic blanket on the grass. It was an orphan's dream.

Through the glass-windowed corridor, I saw Karan returning. I flipped the paper around, scribbled down the phone number and quickly shoved his phone back into his jacket pocket.

TWENTY-SEVEN

That night, before we congregated in the dining room for our evening meal, there was a knock on my bedroom door. I opened it, and was surprised to see my father standing there, holding a white envelope. He almost never came to see me in the privacy of my bedroom; he was very traditional in many ways, and to him, my bedroom was out of bounds, a place for his unmarried daughter, not to be encroached upon by the men of the household. Usually, when he needed to talk to me, he did so in the plain impartiality of our living room.

'Hi, Dad, what's up?' I said, standing in the doorway.

'Sohana, look at this.' He was holding up the envelope. From it, he pulled out two sheets of paper and rustled them in front of me. It was my American Express bill.

'How did you spend more than three lakhs in one week in America?' he asked.

I took the statement from him and glanced

through the charges mindlessly. They were all there: the hotels, the restaurants, the wine bars, the boutiques.

'That's not even counting the airfare,' he said.

I was puzzled. It's not as if our previous overseas excursions had qualified as some backpacking adventure. We always stayed at nice hotels, ate well, shopped with not a great amount of consideration towards the price tags. I didn't understand what my father's issue was, and said as much to him, but in the most respectful way.

'Darling, that is different,' he said, coming in now and sitting down on the chair next to my corner desk. 'When we go on family vacations, or we allow you to go to a friend's wedding – that all is okay, spend and enjoy and be comfortable. But I'm not clear why you even had to make this trip. Mummy tells me you wanted to spend some time with Nitya, that she has been out of sorts. That is good of you, beta, but where was the necessity of spending so much money?'

I wasn't sure what I was feeling next – ashamed that my father had to come in and talk to me like a child or irritated that he felt the need to point out a few expenses which were clearly insignificant in the scheme of things: didn't our family talk in terms of hundreds of millions of dollars? What were a few thousands in comparison?

There was no way I could say what I was thinking without coming across as horribly spoilt.

'When that story came out, Baba had made it clear that nothing was to change,' my father said, speaking to me as if he were a benevolent boarding school headmaster and I some reprobate. 'But he didn't want the family to think that we could spend senselessly, throw money away.'

'But I don't think I did that, Dad,' I said. I hated feeling so … obligated to him, to the rest of the family, for the most fundamental aspects of my life. It became glaringly clear to me, though, that without the Badshah name, the Badshah money, I really wasn't much of anything.

I took the credit card statement from him and started going down the list, justifying what had been spent where, and why. My father stopped me.

'I didn't come here to make you feel bad,' he said. 'Your mother and I have always wanted you to have the best that we could give you. But we never know where life takes us. Today, with God's grace, there is plenty of money. Tomorrow, who knows? We don't know which house you will marry into, what your husband and in-laws will have. People around us are spending like mad, but your mummy and I have always said, let us learn to live with less. So, just be a little thoughtful, a little cautious, haan?'

He was standing now, and reached out and placed his hand gently on my cheek. I lowered my head. He pulled his hand away and left the room.

A few days later, I came home from the gym to find my father and Armaan in serious conversation in the balcony. Armaan looked ashen. His eyes were bleary and red. If I didn't know him better, I would have thought that he'd been crying.

'What happened?' I asked, still clutching my tote, and in desperate need of a shower.

They stared vacantly at me.

'*What?*' I yelled. They were startled. 'Stop treating me like an idiot! I'm not a child! I'm a member of this family! Can you people *please* tell me what is going on?'

I stunned myself with my outburst. My gym bag was on the floor now, at my feet. Chanoo, who had silently appeared with a tray of drinks and evening snacks, hurried off, as if she had been caught intruding upon some inviolable privacy.

Armaan and Dad looked up at me, their faces glazed. Then they looked at each other, as if silently consulting with each other as to what they should do next.

'Sit down,' Armaan said.

It turned out Aroon Malik was not the best friend Armaan thought him to be. Armaan had gone to the office that morning, just any workday, only to be informed of urgent phone messages from the manager at his bank. Cheques – written to photographers, freelance graphic designers, copywriters – had bounced.

Aroon Malik, half of Double-A Ads, had used his corporate signing privileges and raided the company bank account. He had planned it well enough for the funds to have been wired offshore. He was gone, as was all the cash that Double-A had at its disposal. There was nothing left. The authorities had been alerted, a trace put on the money. But Armaan said he harboured little hope of seeing it – or his partner – ever again.

'Oh God,' I said, taking it all in. 'What now?'

Armaan looked over at our father, and then back at me.

'I don't know yet.'

Later, I knocked on Armaan's bedroom door. He didn't shout to me to come in, but I cracked open the door and peered inside. He was lying on the bed, thick padded headphones on his ears. He saw me and pulled the headphones off. It broke my heart to see how defeated my self-sufficient, funny, irascible big brother looked. I hated Aroon Malik for what he had done to him.

'I'm so sorry about everything,' I said. 'Please, Ba, tell me what I can do. There must be something.'

'I am thinking of starting over. The expansion will have to be put on hold, but I have all the contacts, and the reputation. People know that I won't screw them. I always do a good job. Aroon is gone, but I still have everything I had when I started. It will take time, but I can do it.'

'Why do I get the feeling that there's a "but" coming?' I asked.

He got up and began walking around the room. He was still fully dressed in his office gear, still had his shoes on.

'I'm planning on proposing to Ekta,' he said. 'I've already told Mum and Dad.'

'Oh,' I said, thickly. I didn't want to admit to feeling left behind, but that's exactly how I felt. Like everyone else was moving forward with their lives, pairing up, making plans.

He came closer and held my hand.

'I know I'm expected to wait till you are married,' he said. 'But I just don't want this hanging around any more.'

'I know,' I said quietly. 'So propose. Just do it.'

He dropped my hand, started walking around the room again.

'I want to move out. Get Ekta and me our own place.'

My face fell. Even though I didn't see my big brother as often as I would've liked to, it was still comforting to know that his room was down the hall from mine. That he would eventually show up, smelling of cigarettes and whisky, and ruffle my hair as if I were six and not twenty-six. I couldn't imagine being in our house without him.

'With everything the way it is now, I don't know how I can do that, how I can provide for her,' Armaan continued. 'I don't want her to have to work any more. And I refuse to live on what we get from Baba. I won't feel like a man if I did that.'

'So what are you thinking?' I asked. I heard a phone ring somewhere in the house. It was late. The night was drawing to a close.

'I'm thinking that maybe I should put off rebuilding my ad agency for now. That I should accept Baba's invitation. His challenge.'

Armaan had nailed it. That was exactly what the purport of Baba's edict had been. It was a challenge for the most ambitious, most assertive, most forward-thinking grandson to make himself known. All along, I had never imagined it to be Armaan. But as I sat there looking at him, and noticed the new resolve in his eyes, all I could think was: why not?

'Let me help you,' I said.

'You're very sweet, Sohana. But, really, what can *you* do?'

'You would be surprised,' I replied.

TWENTY-EIGHT

If my father could have, he would have sent Aroon Malik a gift basket and a note thanking him for the embezzlement. Although he would never say it out loud, he saw Aroon's nefarious actions as something of a blessing. By taking off with the money in Double-A's bank accounts, disabling the business, Aroon had inadvertently done my father a great service. Jeetu Badshah's secret and most ardent wish was for his oldest child – and, really, his only truly eligible offspring as far as inheriting the business went – to have a shot at helming the empire. Without Armaan, he had no hope. I was a girl and Rajan a child. If Armaan didn't throw his hat into the ring, our particular branch of the Badshah family business would have no chance whatsoever to claim the legacy that was its to inherit.

Armaan had clearly talked to my father before breakfast the next morning. Because by the time the bowls of khichdi and platters of freshly fried papad were being laid out, the two were holding pens over sheets of lined yellow paper in an early morning father–son brainstorming session.

'Baba said to be bold,' Armaan recalled. 'What do you think that means?'

'I think he wanted you to do something different. That was how Baba became who he is. He took risks,' answered my father.

I pulled up a chair and joined them. For once, nobody stopped talking when I showed up.

Armaan was doodling on his pad.

'The food business is always good,' he said. 'Didn't you say once that you can't go wrong providing food to the masses? Everybody needs it. Don't we own agricultural land? Instead of selling the harvests to wholesalers, why can't we take control of it ourselves? We could set up factories, baking bread using the wheat we grow, package our own rice and grains. There's no end to what we could do.'

'Not exciting enough,' I said, unbidden, while scooping seeds out of a papaya.

They both turned distractedly to look at me.

'Sure, you could start a supermarket chain, or find a way to manufacture cheap edibles. But others are already doing it.' I rattled off a list of families in the food business. 'A *lot* of people are doing it. It's not audacious enough. You know what I think? That article didn't make Badshah

Industries look very good. It might have been impressive, the talk of all that money, but the company came across as being disreputable. I think that's what angered Baba most. And now he's asking the boys to come up with something so unique that everyone will forget whatever underhand dealings the company might have had in the past. He wants his name to be cleared. And baking bread isn't going to do that.'

Dad and Armaan gaped at me. They couldn't deny that there was more than an iota of truth in what I was saying. I realized that they didn't even know that it was the truth until they heard it.

Armaan scratched out everything he had written on his notepad.

'Okay, Sis. Seeing that you're the expert here – what do you think I should do?'

I reconsidered doing so a hundred times, but the next day, I called Jag.

'Remember how you said you owed me?'

'Of course,' he replied.

'Okay. I need something. Better than the microscopic solar chip. I need a lead, a big one.'

'Who is this for?' he asked, his voice quiet, serious. There were people in the background. He was busy.

I thought about his question for a minute,

thought about the big brother I needed to help, the one to whose wrist I had tied a raakhi for more than two decades, ever since I could hold a string in my chubby little baby fingers.

'It's for me,' I said.

'Really?' he asked. He sounded heartened, elated.

'Look. It's my brother, okay? He had never been interested in the business. Things have changed. He has a girlfriend. He wants to give it a shot. And I want to help him.'

'So I should help you help your brother?' Jag asked.

'Actually, yes,' I said, a little defensively.

'You know what I think, Sohana? I think you, yourself, need to give this a go, but you're too scared. I'm telling you that you don't have to be. I'm here. I'm with you. Just because I can't marry you doesn't mean I can't help you. You have what it takes to be your own woman, Sohana. Forget your brothers and your cousins. Shock everyone. Win the company.'

I then did something I'd never done to Jag before, and something I thought I would never ever, in a million years, do. I hung up on him.

The next day, I sat looking at the scrap of paper on which I had written R. Dutta's phone number.

Before what had happened between Armaan and Aroon, I had planned to hand it over to Milan. Karan was up to something – I wasn't sure what – that didn't sit right.

Ravi Dutta. Son of a leading industrialist. A bonafide man-about-town. He had a receding hairline, small teeth, a giant stock portfolio. He always had at least three black-clad girls hanging off his arms at parties. According to Nitya, my personal Page Three reporter, Ravi had fallen out of favour with his father after making a series of mistakes that had almost cost Chandru Dutta his fortune. The word doing the rounds was that Chandru was now much closer to his stepson Samir who was being groomed to take over the business. Which left Ravi, according to Nitya, absolutely nowhere.

It seemed that Karan and Ravi were planning something, something that had to do with getting financing from the biggest bank in the country. And, as I thought about it some more, I realized that the only reason two scions of cash-rich companies would need to lobby for capital would be because whatever they were planning had nothing do with the family business, because whatever they were doing had to be kept under wraps. And just a week earlier, I believed that Milan needed to see it.

But everything had changed now. As Armaan had said that night after the dinner at Baba's, business is a changing game, and the players can change too. I just had to be clear about whose team I was going to be on.

I flipped the scrap of paper around again. The crayon drawing was still there, as fresh as the day it was made. A little girl in front of a red-roofed house. A stick figure father and mother. Food. That was all the orphan girl had wanted. A place to live. People to love her. Food to fill her tummy. I suddenly felt sick about what I had agreed to do. I folded the page, went to my closet, found the black lacquered box that held all my keepsakes, and put the drawing inside.

TWENTY-NINE

'Really?' said Milan. 'There's like a bloody hundred movies to watch and you want to see a film about some phirangi who can't talk?'

We were at Inox, waiting for *The King's Speech* to start, and Milan was bemoaning the fact that he was there. He was, after all, the sort of boy who thought *Alien vs Predator* was haute cinema.

'It won a bunch of Oscars,' I insisted.

'I don't want to watch an Oscar film. I don't want to think,' he said, breaking off a piece from the Cadbury Fruit & Nut bar I offered him. 'I've had a shitty day.'

'Why, what happened?' I asked.

'The markets were down. And there was some health violation at the restaurant I co-own in Bangalore. I told my manager to just pay the official off, be done with it.'

'How are things with Anushka?' I enquired.

His face softened.

'She's really great, Soh. I think I'm totally

falling for her. But dude, her schedule is crazy. She left for Zurich yesterday for a shoot, then Sydney after that. She's hanging out with these goddamn movie heroes all day long. It's making me go nuts because I want to be with her, and I can't.' He looked more serious about her than I'd ever seen him about any other woman. Here he was, in love with a gorgeous actress, while my brother wanted to marry a supermodel. Poor Jaanvi would be out-glammed and outshone at every Badshah gathering unto eternity.

'Listen, Milan, I need to tell you something,' I said.

'Now what?' he asked. He did not look like he was in the mood to listen to anything.

'I've just been thinking, you know, about what you asked me to do.' I lowered my voice. 'The spying.'

'Yeah, so?'

'I'm done,' I said. 'I'm not going to do it any more. You have some information about what Sharan is up to. Karan – I couldn't get anything from him. Pawan is off-limits, you said. And there's something else.'

He stared at me blankly. I didn't think he wanted to hear further.

'Armaan has decided he wants to have a shot as well. Something has happened at his business.

It's kind of fallen apart. So that leaves him with time, and motivation.'

'So let me guess,' Milan said, switching off his cell phone. 'You're going to help him. And because you're helping him, you can't help me.'

'I'm sorry, Milan, but he's my brother. Whatever I can do for him, I will do. But I'm not going to tell him what you or anybody else in the family is up to. So I think you should agree not to ask me what he's planning either. I think all of you should just do your best and see where things go. Nobody should have an unfair advantage. It's just not right.'

The lights dimmed. The trailers began.

I was back at Matunga Dada's. This time it was I, not Preeti, who had stopped to buy his favourite cashew barfi. He was as happy as ever to see me, and greeted me with a tiny teaspoon of jal from a small silver cup plucked from his shrine. I went there, I realized, because there was nowhere else I wanted to go.

'How is the family?' he asked. It was as if he was talking about *a* family and not *his* family.

'Everyone is fine,' I said at first. Then, not convinced with my answer, I added, 'Actually, Dada, everyone is not fine.'

He moved a stack of newspapers off the couch.

'Sit,' he said. 'Tell me.'

I didn't even know where to start. The beginning – that front page – seemed like such a long time ago. Until I realized that that wasn't even the beginning. That whatever was happening within the family, the *avarice* that seemed to have taken root in the Badshah household, had probably always been there, dormant. But still, I talked to Dada about everything: the newspaper story, Baba's summary dismissal of his three sons when it came to inheriting the company, the offers he had recieved to sell the business and his ill-conceived decision to let the grandsons fight over it instead.

But I didn't stop there: limbered by two cups of hot tea and Dada's steady, sympathetic gaze, I told him about Jag, how he had left me in London, the lawsuit between his father and Amit Uncle and the information that had come to light since then.

All of it tumbled out of my mouth. And then I stopped, exhausted. My mouth was dry from all the talking.

Matunga Dada said nothing: his long, knobbly fingers were placed under his chin, as if he were a $100-an-hour therapist and I a moderately disturbed patient. He gazed at me. And then a big smile spread across his face, as though he had barely heard a word of what I had said.

'You have shared a lot with me today,' he said. 'You have come all the way here, and I won't let you leave empty handed.'

He rose from his weathered seat and wandered off. My only thought was that he was going to return with a piece of jewellery or a small gold coin – my family was big on gold coins. There was a communal cache perpetually being re-gifted from one family member to another.

Instead, he came back with the scroll from his cabinet, the one I had seen weeks ago, of the drawing he had made when he was a young man. He put it down on the table between us.

'There are things I have told nobody,' he said. 'Things that would have gone to the grave with me. But here you sit, my favourite grandniece, distressed and confused, and it saddens an old man's heart to see that happening. But you must swear not to repeat what I tell you to another soul.'

I nodded. My heart was racing furiously. What was happening?

'Take this when you go,' he said, placing the scroll on my lap. 'Let it serve as a reminder that things are rarely as they seem. That *people*, my dear, are rarely as they seem.'

He gulped down the rest of his tea. And then it was his turn to talk.

When I left Dada's, I was so preoccupied that I had to be mindful of where I placed my foot next, lest I end up in a heap at the bottom of the rickety steps. In my other hand, I was clutching the scroll he had given me, careful not to squeeze it too hard.

I remembered the picture in the newspaper article, the one of a slender-limbed Baba as a twenty-year-old man, working in a steel mill. He was 'completely self-made', the article had said.

If only.

THIRTY

Pawan dropped by my house the next day. Despite the time it took to negotiate the hideous bumper-to-bumper traffic in the city, my relatives tended to drop in on one another with alarming frequency. Still, I was surprised to see him at our home, alone, without his brother. He had come on the pretext of bringing my mother a parcel of goodies that she had requested from Singapore, and which had been carted back to Indian shores by a friend of his.

When it was just Pawan and me standing in the foyer, he asked if we could talk.

'Sure,' I said, leading him into the balcony. 'What's up?'

'Ever since Baba said what he did – that all of us have the right to try and win the business – I've been working hard. Really hard.'

'That's great, Pawan. You've always been the smart one in the family.'

He blushed a little, removed his glasses, wiped

them on the front of his shirt and peered through them to check for any remaining flecks of dust before slipping them back on.

'UAVs,' he said. Noticing the blank look on my face, he clarified, 'Unmanned Aerial Vehicles. Basically, planes that fly without anyone piloting them. One of the new technological advancements that should be explored.'

'Okay,' I said. 'Sounds good.'

'They have crucial military applications, and Badshah, as a company, has not yet investigated the potential of defence contracts. The Ministry of Defence has already said it will use more home-grown companies instead of awarding contracts to Israel or America. So why not us? Why not Badshah?'

'Fair question,' I said, still puzzled as to why he was telling me all that. 'Pawan, have you talked to your dad about it? He would be the best person to advise you.'

My cousin shook his head.

'I can't,' he said. 'This decision of Baba's has really affected him. He's depressed. He goes in to work but his mind is not there. He feels, what is the point if he will be thrown out anyway ...'

'I just don't know if I'm the person you should be consulting,' I confessed. 'I really don't know much about any of it.'

Pawan cocked his head and looked at me thoughtfully.

'That's not true, Sohana. I know you have been helping Milan. He told me.'

'Then maybe you should talk to *him* about this?'

I was now tired of being dragged into it all; these five boys, their random ideas, their pitches for greatness. I just wanted to be left out of it.

'Tell me what you think,' he said. 'And then I will go to Milan with it. Once I complete my research with due diligence and ascertain how realistic it is, what the logistics are, I'm going to give the idea to my brother. It will be his.'

'What?' I said. 'Why?'

'Because he's my older brother, and I can see him running Badshah more than I can see myself doing it.'

I took a deep breath. I had become a confidante, a sounding board, to the boys. I had always wanted to be included, and now that I was, I wasn't quite sure what to do.

'In the first place, Pawan, Milan is *ninety-three* seconds older than you. That's it. Second, there's no reason why you can't have a shot at taking over. You have as much right as he does.'

'But I thought you'd be happy,' Pawan said, seeming a little disappointed with my response.

'Everyone knows how tight you and Milan are.'

I moved closer to him and put my hand on his arm.

'Yes, that's true. But *you're* my cousin too. Milan has had plenty of advantages in his life. He doesn't need to take something else from you.'

I was staring at the boy whose only brother wanted me to spy on him, to steal his ideas. It was only now, in the wake of my conversation with Matunga Dada, that I had begun to see how distasteful that was, how cruel Milan could be at times.

'What are you saying?'

'I am saying, Pawan Prakash Badshah, that you can do this. So go do it.'

Ekta, my sister-in-law-to-be, was finally being introduced to the family. Armaan had told my parents about her. My mother, although initially somewhat reserved in her response because she had had no hand in finding the girl her firstborn wanted to marry, ended up dusting one of her old six-carat diamonds and having it sized and set for her new daughter-in-law, in time for the engagement.

That night, my mother had planned to slide onto Ekta's wrist a pair of bangles studded with ruby baguettes, which she had shown me to get my opinion. They were new, glittering in their blue velvet box, elegant and not too showy. As far as a first piece of jewellery went, I told my mother, they were more than adequate.

It was going to be just the five of us and Ekta; Armaan wanted our parents, Rajan and me to meet Ekta before anyone else did. The week after, he planned to take her to see Baba and Dadi, to get their blessings, and then she would be introduced to the rest of the family. As I jokingly told Armaan, if Ekta wasn't scared off by then, she would make a fine addition to the Badshah clan.

Armaan was about to leave to pick her up and bring her home. I went into his room where he was shaving in the en-suite bathroom, the door ajar. Since the Aroon Malik debacle, Double-A Ads had quickly finished off its projects, wriggled out of future obligations and, essentially, ground to a halt. Aroon had not just made off with my brother's earnings and livelihood but, it seemed, his ardour for advertising as well. His attention had shifted now – to the girl he loved, to the business he wanted to seize.

He was holding his razor, a smudge of shaving cream on his left cheek.

'Thanks, Sohana, for everything,' he said, in a

rare, reflective mood. 'You have really helped me. That idea you gave me is fantastic.'

'You are welcome, Ba,' I said. 'I just want to see you happy.'

I thought back to my last conversation with Jag, when I had hung up on him. He had called me back the next day, apologetic, and promised never to chide me about playing second fiddle to my cousins and brother. He agreed to help me.

'LNG,' Jag had said.

'Huh?'

Sometimes he forgot that I was not part of his world.

'Sorry. Liquefied natural gas. World demand for it is soaring and will only rise in the years to come. It's a clean source of energy, with just half the emissions of coal. There's a plant in Azerbaijan, where there's a large, proven natural gas reserve. But they're not exporting in high volumes yet, largely because of issues with the infrastructure and lack of capital.'

'So what can Armaan do?' I asked.

'He needs to find a way to enter the game. If he makes a significant enough investment in the plant, he can control the exports to India. He can collaborate with a maritime agency that has specially outfitted ships.'

My head was throbbing. Why couldn't we

have gone with my original plan to bring Harvey Nichols to Mumbai? Wouldn't that have been more fun than liquefied natural gas?

I had told Armaan what Jag had suggested, and my brother was excited enough to start looking into it. But right then, all he wanted to do was go and fetch Ekta.

THIRTY-ONE

Ekta loved the food. She loved my parents. She seemed to love me. Before dinner, she sat next to Rajan on the couch and showed him some game apps he'd never known of. She had a nephew this age, she told us. She had taught him how to skateboard. An hour after she had got to our place, it was clear that the boys of the house were smitten by her.

She was, in person, less 'model-ly' looking than I remembered. In the vodka campaign, her hair had been long and full, flapping in the synthetic wind of the photography studio. In reality, she wore her hair cropped short and her bangs highlighted chestnut brown. She was chic, and casually yet exquisitely put together. Armaan couldn't take his eyes off of her, rushing to refill her glass of water, pulling out a chair for her at the table, gushing to my parents about Ekta's numerous accomplishments – the cover of *Elle*, a deal with Lakme, an upcoming Emanuel Ungaro couture show in Paris. My mother was full of encouragement and praise. When Ekta stood, she was only a couple of inches shorter than Armaan, the pair of them standing there like graceful, well-groomed gazelles. If I were to go by looks alone, I'd say they were perfect for each other.

And she asked questions too. Lots of them. As she tucked into her second helping of the salmon baked in phyllo with champagne sauce I had made – mystifying me as to where all those calories went – she asked me about my time in London, my mother about what she did with her days and Rajan about his school. She was curious about the extended family members as well: what Baba and Dadi were like. She had read the article, of course – 'Who hasn't after all?' she had said, with a flick of her manicured hands, and also commented 'how *fascinating*' it was. She looked around the room as if trying to reconcile herself to the relative lack of ostentation of our home, as if wondering why the chandelier wasn't made of diamonds and no gold covered the walls. It was as if she was expecting us to have the peacock-swagger of a Donald Trump, and seemed mildly disappointed that we weren't that kind of people.

'Tell us about your family,' my father asked her.

'My father is in Baroda,' she said. 'He teaches

music, mostly the sarod and sitar. He wanted me
to learn, but I never quite had the aptitude for it.
My mother died when I was fifteen.'

'I'm sorry,' my father said. 'How?'

'Car accident. She wasn't even driving. She
died on impact. Horrible.' Ekta shook her head,
looked downwards at her plate. Armaan put his
arm around her shoulders comfortingly.

'It's fine,' she said, smiling again. 'It was a very
long time ago.'

'And siblings?' my mother asked.

'Two sisters,' Ekta replied. 'One older, one
younger. Both married with kids, living in Baroda.
They look after Dad, make sure he doesn't get too
lonely.'

'And you came to Mumbai alone?' I asked.

'Yes, alone. But I have friends here. By the time
I was eighteen, I was five-foot-ten, and realized
that maybe I could be a model. I was very much
into books and literature as a child. I thought I
might become a teacher. But people said I should
try modelling. I had to move to Mumbai for that.
I was helped by some acquaintances. I still share
a flat with an old friend. I am able to send money
back to my father. It's a good life that I've made.'

I stared at her. Flawless and smart, and literate
to boot. If I let myself, I could really hate her.

Chanoo came in to ask if we were done.

Mother told her to clean up and serve dessert in the living room. I watched Armaan help Ekta out of her chair. He held her hand and led her down the hallway.

I didn't know what it was, but something didn't sit right. As gracious and beautiful as Ekta was, saying and doing all the right things, something about her didn't ring true. Like it was all rehearsed and she wasn't really the woman she was projecting herself to be. It was the way her eyes wandered when one of us was speaking to her, as if she was eager to leap to the next subject, the next person on the table. As if she was eager to see if she could find something better out there.

But I told myself to stop thinking that way, that it was most likely some residual Jag-related hurt, that seeing my brother so happy and in love only served to remind me of what I didn't have. Armaan was right; Ekta was a good girl. The right girl. He had chosen well.

My layered tiramisu cake had come out beautifully and had been placed atop the coffee table, small plates and tiny forks to its side.

'Sohana made this especially for you,' my mother told Ekta proudly.

'How *lovely!*' she cooed. 'And I so enjoyed the salmon as well. You are quite the cook, aren't you?' she said. Was she being patronizing?

'It just goes to show that we all have our gifts, don't we? Interior design didn't work out for you – but look at you now! You can make tiramisu!' she tittered.

After everyone had enjoyed a slice or two, my mother excused herself for a moment and returned with the blue velvet box. Ekta's eyes lit up at the prospect of receiving something that came in so regal-looking a package. Mom sat down next to her.

'This is the first time you have come to our home. We want to give you something to welcome you into the family, and to thank you for making our son so happy.' She opened the box and pulled out the ruby bangles, which she slid onto Ekta's slender wrists.

'Thank you so much, Aunty,' came an excited reply. Ekta kissed my mother on both cheeks. Then she went over to my father and thanked him as well. She clutched her newly adorned wrist close to her heart, and went back to her place on the sofa, her face frozen in a smile.

After Armaan left to drop Ekta home and the rest of the family was in bed, I went to my closet and fetched the big poster board that I had dragged out weeks earlier, on which I had written the names of the potential heirs to the Badshah empire, and the pros and cons of them being so anointed. Staring at it now, I realized that those qualifications had changed. Sharan's name had had a big star next to it – he had, after all, earned the right to take over. But since Baba had changed the game, Sharan had retreated into his own world. He had alienated himself. He barely came to Baba's dinners anymore, and when he did, he was on the phone the entire time he wasn't at the table. Jaanvi had been looking increasingly unhappy, and I had the feeling that there was something disconcertingly murky going on beneath the surface of their marriage as well as behind whatever Sharan's bid for the business was.

And it seemed that whatever wedge had been driven between Sharan and the rest of the Badshahs had lodged itself between him and his brother too. Since that day at the Byculla orphanage, when I had sneakily checked Karan's call-list, he and I had barely spoken. Jaanvi had told me that her brother-in-law was almost always out of town, signing deals in Delhi, jumping on a plane to Bangkok or Shanghai, telling the family only that it was 'business'.

Milan too had pulled away from me. As soon as I told him that I was going to do what I could for Armaan, my cousin had distanced himself. It seemed as if he saw my siding with my brother as the ultimate act of treachery.

All I wanted to do – what I should have made clear from the very beginning – was to stand back and let them all figure things out on their own. They didn't need me. It was time for this bunch of self-obsessed boys to start acting like men.

I stared at the board again. I uncapped my pen and began to write out what, as far as I knew, my cousins were exploring. There was cold fusion, microscopic solar chips, hydrogen-powered cars, the financing of an off-the-wall movie, liquefied natural gas, a bid for what was surely a serious amount of capital, and unmanned aerial vehicles. It was not bad for a month's work. And amongst these, somewhere, must surely lie the idea that would propel Badshah to the next level, give its reputation a makeover, reinstate its standing in the wider business community. One of these boys would win. And because there still wasn't a frontrunner, it could be anybody.

THIRTY-TWO

'Are you sure you know what you're doing?' I asked Armaan.

He and I had gone for a stroll around Hanging Gardens. We were circling the fountains, the spotlights red with rust. It was early evening and the moon-shaped lamps were aglow. There was something about going there together that reconnected us to each other; it was a favourite family destination when we were children, our mother chasing us both down the cobbled paths, my big brother and I screeching gleefully atop the Boot House and gazing, mesmerized, at leafy green elephants, horses and camels.

'I'm a grown man,' he said. 'Of course I know.'

'It's just that everything is happening so quickly,' I said to him. 'Maybe you should get to know her more before you make such a huge commitment.'

He stopped walking and swivelled around to look at me.

'Why? Didn't you like her?' he asked, his tone accusatory, disbelieving. How could *anyone* not like his Ekta? 'Because she loved you guys. She's going to be a great addition to the family. Trust me.'

He started walking again.

'You only met her a few months ago,' I said. 'A lot of crazy stuff has happened recently. And, you know, you just want to be sure that she wants to be with you for the right reasons.'

'Sohana, I'm not going to have this conversation with you.' Armaan was defensive now. 'And,' he said, 'maybe you should be honest about what your real problem is here. That I'm getting married. And you're not.'

It was as if his words stung him as much as they did me. He paused, a stricken look on his face. It was not like him to be cruel, ever.

'I'm sorry, sis. I shouldn't have said that.' He put his arm around my shoulder. I leaned into him, grateful for the warm solidity of him, grateful for *him*.

I decided to drop it. It shouldn't have been my concern in the first place. He was a street-smart twenty-seven-year-old who had run his own successful business for years. He had always had sharp instincts about people. If he had decided that Ekta was the girl for him, I wasn't going to –

perhaps shouldn't have tried to – convince him otherwise.

I let him lead me to the car. We walked in silence. I loved my brother dearly.

Whatever was going to happen was going to happen.

Dome, on the rooftop of the Intercontinental Hotel, had to be just about the sexiest spot in the city. When Jag and I were together, I had dreamt of taking him there one day. We would sink into the soft white cloud-like couches, gaze at each other over the candles that flickered in small glass jars and clutch miniature pillows to our chests as we spoke quietly, intimately. We would order Roberto Cavalli vodka and Kir Royales, pan-tossed Brazilian tenderloin and honey toasted chicken, and look out over the Indian Ocean and at the skyscrapers along Nariman Point. I would visit the place with Jag and we would talk about our future – one that now, it was evident, would not ever include him.

I was, instead, there with Milan. He had called me that morning, apologizing for being, in his words, 'such a dickhead'. He wanted to make it up to me.

We talked like we used to before all the nastiness, before the article, before Baba threw down the gauntlet and willed his grandsons to crush each other in their bid to pick it up. For a blissful hour, we didn't even talk about the family, or Anushka, or hydrogen-powered vehicles or solar anything. We gossiped and giggled, him teasing me good-naturedly about how I'd only ever learned to design 'a third of a house', and me playfully mocking him about the muscle tee and rapper-inspired low-slung jeans he was wearing.

'I'm really sorry, Soh,' he said, turning serious. 'I should never have asked you to do something you didn't feel right about. You're my sister. I shouldn't have expected you to do my dirty work. You're better off not getting involved.'

'It's okay,' I said. 'I think we all got carried away. Baba put you boys in a terrible position. Everyone was desperate. I understand that now.'

Someone walked in, a handsome figure in a white shirt and dark jeans. He made his way to the corner of the bar and sat at a table behind a potted plant. He didn't see us.

'Look, it's Sharan,' I said to Milan, pointing in our cousin's direction. I stood up. 'Shall we go say hello?'

Milan grabbed my hand, yanked me back to my seat.

'Wait,' he said. He was craning his neck, trying to see beyond the leafy fronds.

'Who's he with?' Milan asked, squinting.

I leaned backwards, trying to look discreetly. I noticed the bob first, sleek and shiny.

'Mary, his secretary,' I replied.

'Crap! Really? What are they doing?'

'Just talking,' I said. That was true, but there was something in the way they talked that made me stare at them a little longer. Sharan was smiling, leaning attentively towards her, as if adoring her every word. On the table between them lay a couple of files and a notepad. Mary was holding a pen. It was contrived, as if they were in a play, and the stationery was nothing more than a prop. It was as if Mary had put it all out to make it look like it was some kind of a conference. But Dome was not the place to talk business – lots of other kinds of talk, but not business.

'If he was really messing around with her, they wouldn't come here, would they?' I asked Milan. 'It's so public.'

'Maybe,' my cousin replied. 'Or maybe Sharan just doesn't care any more.'

Sharan glanced around his side of the bar, as if checking to see if he recognized anyone. He nodded to Mary who lifted her pert little bottom off the couch, came around to Sharan's side, and slid in next to him. Their thighs were touching.

'Considering he's her boss, she's sitting pretty close to him,' I reported to Milan. 'Yup, something's going on.'

'Like mother, like son, right?' Milan said.

On the way home, I wondered if I should tell Jaanvi. But tell her what? That her husband was having a drink at Dome with his secretary? That they were sitting next to each other on a big, comfortable couch? I couldn't tell her about the feeling, the instinct of mine, because she didn't know me well enough to trust my instincts. Even if we were friendlier now than we had ever been, we weren't close in the way I was with Nitya or Milan. Since lunch at her house, I'd gone with her to pick out a new stone Ganesha for the temple at her home, and introduced her to the top teacher – with whom Jaanvi wanted private lessons – at one of Nitya's yoga studios. But I didn't want to get into this murky business. As Milan said, it was better for me to not get involved.

THIRTY-THREE

There was no more cranberry juice at Baba's house, a fact that seemed to cause Amit Uncle no end of anxiety. He yelled at the servant when told that Malini could not have the Cosmopolitan she wanted.

'How long will it take you to go out and buy cranberry juice?' he said as he pulled a wad of notes out of his pocket. 'Here! Go! Now!'

Everyone turned to stare. Malini looked embarrassed. Amit Uncle, as we could all see, was drunk.

'My wife wants what she wants!' he shouted. 'Don't you, darling?' he said, turning to look at her.

My mother gently pulled him to one side. 'Bhau, come with me,' she said softly. 'We'll have some coffee in the kitchen.'

I stared at Malini who sat perched on the edge of an armchair. She looked stricken and was quiet, her mind elsewhere. None of the brash humour or outrageous innuendo she would fling our way at usual family get-togethers.

Barely anyone had made it to dinner that night. It was, in my recollection, the thinnest crowd at Baba's house ever. Sharan was working late, which Milan interpreted as him 'boning his secretary'. Karan was travelling again. Armaan was with Ekta, Jaanvi home with a headache. Pawan was with a student. Preeti was in the kitchen, checking on dinner. Rajan was around, but at that moment kicking a ball outside with a boy from the house next door.

Even Baba and Dadi hadn't made their appearance yet.

'What's the deal with Amit Uncle?' Milan asked of Prakash Chacha.

'Your guess is as good as mine,' our youngest uncle said, shrugging. 'He's been in a bad mood all afternoon. I don't know what's bugging him.'

'Things must be stressful, right?' I asked him. 'Like, at work? All the uncertainty.'

'It's not easy, no,' Prakash Chacha said. 'Depending on what happens with the business, whom it ultimately goes to, your father and Amit and I could be out of work in a few months.' He paused, picking out a spicy twig from a bowl of chivda. 'It's not about the money,' he said. 'It's never been the money. It's about having something that belonged to us. I thought this company did. Until Baba told us it didn't.'

His honesty was heartbreaking – not just had he shed the bravado that he and his brothers had been hiding behind all the time, he had also pierced through to the heart of the matter: something was being taken away from him. From all of them. From all of us, except one.

Some perverse logic had gripped Baba, some senseless vengeance. In the light of what Matunga Dada had told me, Baba's actions seemed almost criminal. But my great-uncle had sworn me to secrecy. There was nothing more I could do.

The TV was playing in a corner of the room, the sound barely audible. Prakash, Milan and I stared at the screen, wordlessly.

'Chacha, what do you know about that court case with Balu Sachdev?' The question was sudden, and seemingly out of nowhere. Milan whipped his head in my direction, astonished. It looked as if he'd thought I'd forgotten all about it and had put it behind me. I thought I had too. Until I realized I had the opportunity – a passing moment with a kindly uncle in an otherwise busy and crowded life, at a time when he was being open and honest; I had to jump at it. I was never going to get the truth from a source closer than that.

'How do you know about that?' he asked, frowning – more out of curiosity than anger.

'It was in the newspaper,' I said.

'Why are you so interested?'

'I sort of know the family,' I replied, vaguely. 'I met them while I was in London.'

'They are good people,' Prakash Chacha said. He reached for the remote control and turned the TV off. Then he turned his attention back to me.

'What happened was not Sachdev's fault,' he continued. 'We had an agreement, and he fulfilled his end of the bargain. He bought the land because we – Amit, actually – promised to get the financing to help him develop it.'

'So what happened?'

'Amit changed his mind. No, I take that back. *Baba* changed his mind. Nothing happens at Badshah Industries without Baba knowing about it. By the time the land was acquired and Amit started lining up investors, the property market in the US crashed. Baba was no longer interested. It didn't matter that he had given another man his word.'

'But the newspaper said that Balu Sachdev won in court.'

'Baba will see to it that Sachdev never gets a single paisa,' my uncle said. 'Your grandfather would rather pay an army of lawyers to hold the case up forever than admit that we did anything wrong.'

'So we just do nothing and let an innocent man lose everything?'

'Beta,' Prakash Chacha said. 'In Baba's view of the world, there is no such thing as an innocent man.'

The doors to the living room opened. My grandparents stood at the entrance, looking around.

'Where is everyone?' Dadi asked.

Dinner was quiet. The table was only half-full, but there was as much food on it as ever. Malini didn't touch anything on her plate. Amit Uncle looked as if he had sobered up, but his eyes were still bloodshot. He drank only ice water. And he and his wife didn't even glance at each other all through the meal.

Baba had already been briefed as to who was where – the overseas trips, the more important engagements.

'I hear that our Armaan has chosen a girl,' Baba said now, looking at my parents.

'Yes, we have met her. They will come to seek your blessings,' my mother said.

'And when, exactly, do they plan on doing that?' Baba asked, a bitter tone in his voice. 'It seems that the whole town knows more about it than I do.'

'Sorry, Baba,' Dad said. 'Armaan has been tied up due to an unfortunate turn of events to do with his business.'

'Yes, I have heard about his friend. The chor.'

Baba always knew just the right thing to say.

'Tell me about the girl,' he said. 'Who are the parents?'

My mother began recounting Ekta's story but couldn't finish before Rajan chimed in with his own pre-pubescent opinion.

'She's awesome, Baba,' my little brother said enthusiastically. 'She's really good at Plants versus Zombies!'

Baba ignored his youngest grandson and turned his attention back to my parents.

'I am not sure a fashion model is the best sort of girl for our family,' Baba said. 'This business of undressing in front of strangers. Showing off before the cameras. These are not the kind of values we have.'

My parents glanced at each other. I know that deep down, they shared the same concerns; that if they could have picked, they would have opted for a daughter-in-law with a lifestyle somewhat less overt. But they were trying to be supportive, I could tell. And, more than that, to be hip. These days, in the circles in which they moved, that seemed more important than anything.

'The plan is for Ekta to give up this line of work once she and Armaan marry,' Mom said, although I wasn't sure from where she gleaned that particular nugget of information. As far as I could recall, Ekta had said no such thing. 'At the end of the day, she is a sweet and simple girl.'

I turned my head towards Milan and rolled my eyes. If Ekta was sweet and simple, I was Lady Gaga.

'I will judge that for myself when I meet her,' Baba said, a little ominously. 'Tell that son of yours to bring her to me.'

Dessert was brought out; small silver cups, their exteriors covered with water droplets, containing freshly churned kulfi, studded with chopped pistachios and laced with saffron. It was one of the few things that Dadi still made herself, and it was as sweet and delicious as it was when she used to feed it to me as a baby.

I scraped the last creamy drop from the bottom of my cup and licked my spoon like a kid.

'More?' Dadi asked me.

I nodded wholeheartedly. Everyone else had gradually left the table.

'Come,' she said.

I followed her into the kitchen where the

servants were scouring the blackened pots and
boiling jasmine petals for Baba's night-time tea.
I listened to the comforting swoosh-swoosh of
the thick straw broom as it brushed across the tile
floor, clearing up the day's debris and dust. The
kitchen would start afresh in the morning.

Dadi opened the freezer, pulled out the
container of kulfi, set it on the counter and started
chipping away at it with a spoon, waiting for
the frozen milky confection to gradually yield
and turn soft and pliant. The frosted tub pressed
briefly against her sari, leaving a small, damp
spot. With her pallav, she wiped off a delicate
row of beads of perspiration that had gathered
above her lip. Prominent matriarch she might
have been, but she still wasn't averse to using an
expensive piece of French chiffon to sop up sweat.
I smiled as I watched her.

She scooped out a healthy portion and
placed it in my bowl. Then she brought out a
small red tin and let some pistachios fall from
it onto a wooden board, and the two of us set
about shelling them, crushing the delicate green
nutmeat with a rolling pin and tossing them into
my dessert. I picked up a spoonful of kulfi and
held it to my grandma's lips. She put her hand
over mine, ate, and fed me back.

'You will never be too old for me to put

something sweet in your mouth,' she said, her voice tender.

A lump formed at the back of my throat. Suddenly, I was five, sitting on her lap, and she was my Dadi, combing my hair, buckling my shoes and kissing my tiny forehead before I ran out to play. As a child, I frequently tripped over a wayward shoe or a toy motorcycle on my way out. Dadi would pick me up, put me back on her knee and kiss my hurt away.

'Don't rush,' she would say. 'Slow and steady wins the race.' It was her favourite saying.

Now she lifted up her hand and put it to my cheek.

'You are my only granddaughter,' she said. 'There were all those boys. And then you. Our Lakshmi.'

I blushed. It had been years since Dadi had spoken to me like that, with so much affection. Still, there was a hint of sorrow in her eyes.

'A good boy will come for you,' she said. 'I promise you that.'

'I know,' I said.

She removed her hand from my cheek, placed it on my arm. Her back stiffened. Her voice changed. Her eyes were clear and bright again.

'But before that, before you lose your Badshah name, you must truly become one.'

I frowned, puzzled.

'I don't understand.'

'Do not discount yourself,' she said. 'Step out of the shadows. Let people see who you really are. You are a Badshah, as much as any of them. Everything can be yours.' She paused. 'Samjhi?'

'Ji, Dadi,' I said, my voice trembling.

THIRTY-FOUR

All the way home, my mind replayed over and over my conversation with Dadi. It had been an unforgettable night: Prakash Chacha admitting to me that Jag's father had been cheated out of what was due to him, Amit Uncle and Malini squabbling worse than I'd ever seen, and then Dadi feeding me some sort of cryptic advice along with a childhood treat.

I called Jag almost as soon as I got home.

'I'm sorry for how my family cheated your father,' I said. 'Hearing Prakash Chacha admit it tonight made it sink in.'

'It was never your fault,' he said. 'I never meant to make you feel as if it was.'

'All this stuff has made me re-evaluate everything,' I said. I was talking to him as I would to Milan or Nitya. I had never thought I could become friends with Jag – he had rejected me, and in so doing, had hurt me in the worst way. But how he was with me now – sympathetic, a caring listener – was Jag at his best, the man who hadn't changed, the man I had fallen for.

'It's great that you're there for your family,' he said. 'It's one of the things I've always loved about you. But, Sohana, you need to get on with your own life as well. You know that, right?'

We said our goodbyes, and I went out into the living room to see if my parents were still up. They were half-watching TV, half-reading the evening papers.

'What was going on with Amit Chacha tonight?' I asked them, sitting next to my mother on the couch.

'He had a bad day at work,' Dad responded.

'Dad, lots of people have bad days. But this was different. He was really mad at Malini Chachi.'

My parents glanced at each other, as if considering how much to tell me, how much they could get away with keeping hidden.

'It is a matter for husband and wife to sort out,' Dad said with finality. He wasn't going to discuss it any more.

'Isn't this Karan's friend?'

Milan tossed the day's business section onto his desk, where I was sitting. I turned the newspaper around so it faced me. There was a photo of Ravi Dutta. The accompanying story said that Dutta, chief operating officer of the publicly listed CDC – Chandru Dutta Corporation – had tendered his resignation, effective immediately. Under Ravi's leadership, CDC, founded by Ravi's father, had been almost driven to financial ruin. The stock prices had nosedived. Manufacturing plants had been shut down. But Chandru Dutta's new stepson, Samir Khan, was a business wunderkind. He had restructured the corporation, eliminated loss-producing endeavours and taken the company back to profit. The share price was climbing back up. And as a result, Samir was in, Ravi out.

I continued reading.

Ravi Dutta declined to comment when contacted for this report. But sources familiar with the inner workings of the company have informed us that Dutta is in talks with a potential new partner and is close to landing significant capital to start his own business or take over an existing one. Indian businesses should be warned: before Dutta joined his father's company, he worked at Wall Street corporate raider Randall Brothers.

'Yes, Karan's friend,' I nodded vaguely.

Manjuli had been texting me twice a day. Then, on a Wednesday morning, she called me, and when I answered the phone, she did not bother to conceal her irritation.

'My editor is growing very impatient,' she said. 'He is pressuring me for the follow-up story.'

'There's nothing to report right now,' I replied.

'He wants to know what's going on,' she said. 'I'm sorry, Miss Badshah, but we cannot wait any more. There is a lot of talk in the market. We have more than enough information from other sources to put together another report. And,' she said, lowering her voice, 'you might also want to know … I have a friend at *Ok!* magazine. She is investigating some rumours regarding, err, *infidelity*, within your family.'

What was Manjuli trying to tell me? That she knew about Malini and Vivek? Sharan and Mary? Or, God forbid, was someone else in the Badshah clan messing around too? And was she claiming to have this knowledge in order to coerce me into telling her something I wasn't ready to share with her yet?

'Miss Badshah? Are you there?' she asked.

'Yes,' I said quietly.

'You just have to understand that the information we need is out there. It is all a matter of how it is presented. There are some things that you can control.' She paused. 'It's your choice.'

'Fine,' I said. 'I'll meet you on Saturday.'

THIRTY-FIVE

Nitya invited me to Ladies' Night at Prive. DJ Aqeel was there, and according to sources at the entrance, Katrina Kaif was to show up too. Nitya wanted to celebrate an offer she had to sell her yoga studios for a surprisingly generous sum. She was already thinking about how she would reinvest her profits, what her next venture would be. I had a new admiration for her.

The music pounded in my ears, leaving me with a slight headache. The dance floor was so packed that I wouldn't have stepped in even if somebody *had* asked me to dance, which was not the case. Instead, Nitya and I sat at our corner table, which was laden with platters of sushi. At various points in the night, several acquaintances came over to say hello: girls clad in halter necks and high heels, all white smiles and frosted lips; boys in black shirts, crisp jeans and wallets padded by their daddies; the girls looking to make a meaningful connection, the boys to get lucky.

Milan's friend Pancho, whom I hadn't seen since the night of my dinner party, was present with a gaggle of rich boys. He sent over a bottle of Moët, and winked at me when the bottle was uncorked. I waved my thanks across the room and raised a glass to him. He had a charming cheekiness to him, a blithe sophistication.

I thought of my driver waiting on the sidewalk outside the Radio Club, a stone's throw away. I wished I was there, playing bingo with my parents like I used to when younger, eating vegetable Manchurian and sticky rice at a table that overlooked the ocean.

Prive, and so many other places like it, had been my wheelhouse. I *belonged* there. But now, an indolent malcontent tapped away at the edges of my being. Amit Uncle's wife was a cheat. Sharan was an adulterer. Armaan was about to marry the wrong girl. Prakash Chacha was on the verge of depression and Milan, although he would never admit it, had started looking desperate. And my grandfather wasn't the man I had always thought him to be.

The champagne was drained now, little sips taken by all who stopped by to say hello.

'Let's go,' I said to Nitya.

'It's barely midnight,' she said, glancing at her watch. 'What's wrong with you?'

'The driver looked tired. I shouldn't keep him out much longer.'

'You're really something,' Nitya replied.

I picked up my purse. I couldn't stay a second longer. I was meeting Manjuli next morning anyway. I wanted to go home and prepare.

'Come,' I said, holding out my hand to my best friend. 'I'll drop you home.'

Outside, we waited for the driver to arrive. Dozens of people had lined up to get into the club. The bald bouncer, a beefy man with a doughy face and squinty eyes, picked and chose who got in by their level of notoriety as a starlet, socialite or business scion. If they were none of those, he let them in or not depending on how cute they were.

'What's going on with you?' Nitya asked. 'You used to *love* this place. I used to have to drag you out at dawn. It is still so early. You want to go somewhere else?'

I wasn't sure what it was, but suddenly, a frisson of cold gripped my heart. I started breathing in short, heavy bursts.

'What's wrong, Soh?' Nitya asked, her eyes wide with concern.

Tears pricked behind my eyes.

'I'm not sure,' I gasped.

'God, Soh, you're like having some kind of a panic attack.'

Another row of cars had pulled up, Porsches and BMWs, each shinier and newer than the next. Doors opened and loud music blared out. Akon. Jay-Z. Kesha. Pounding beats. Excited chatter. Everywhere, there was the smell of new money. This was supposed to be my world. I was Sohana Badshah, the lone granddaughter of the richest family in India. I could have anything. Everyone said I could have any man I wanted. But I couldn't. And here I was, surrounded by people I knew, and I had never felt more alone.

A plane flew overhead. Sirens sounded somewhere in the distance.

I thought of Jag walking out on me. The design course that lay forgotten by the wayside. An abandoned piece of land in New Jersey, a court case without end. Matunga Dada, an old wedding photo, a dust-covered scroll. The truth about Baba.

I had been part of my family for twenty-six years and only now was I learning its secrets.

Nitya stared at me, her eyes wide, mouth agape. She put her hand on the small of my back.

I bent over and focused on my breath. In. Out. Find a rhythm. Slow. Steady. Dadi's favourite saying from my childhood. Slow and steady wins the race.

I hadn't understood it till right at that moment, but I was in a race. Until just a minute ago, I was just another heiress in a town cluttered with them. I closed my eyes for a second and saw how others saw me, how I saw the girls with whom I had come to be lumped: manicured fingers, diamond rings, red-soled shoes and bedazzled Blackberries. We were all the same, a congeneric gathering of young women with tresses dyed brown, brows plucked high, personas scrubbed clean of authenticity. We lived to dress well, marry better, and to inhabit a glossy world padded with superlatives.

I didn't want to be that girl any more.

I *wasn't* that girl any more.

I straightened myself. I pulled my phone out of my purse. I checked my watch and dialled Jag's number. It was noon on Friday in San Francisco. He would be at work.

He answered immediately.

'Hey, Soh, what's up?'

I thought back to my whiteboard, all those names and rationales I had scrawled on it, naively, not so long ago.

With a new lucidity, I saw my brothers for the men they really were, for what would eventually become of Badshah Industries if any of them won it. Sharan would hoard every last piece of it. Karan would let his shady friend step over the threshold. Milan would squander the family fortune in no time and Pawan, if he inherited it, would present it to his twin. My own brother, whether he cared to admit it or not, would let his wife-to-be take over. Ekta had her eye on the prize, and it wasn't Armaan.

'Jag,' I said into the phone, my voice trembling. 'I need to do something.'

He sighed deeply.

'Okay,' he said. 'Talk to me.'

I did. Slowly and steadily.

Find out what happens next in
Bombay Girl, Book Two
Coming soon …

ACKNOWLEDGEMENTS

My enduring gratitude to the fine people at HarperCollins India, led by the brilliantly intuitive V.K. Karthika. Thank you for saying yes.

Many thanks to Prema Govindan for her swift and spot-on editing, and to Lipika Bhushan and Neha Punj for knowing how to get the word out.

To my agent, Jodie Rhodes, who had the foresight to say, 'Do a book just for India. Better still, do three.'

To my dear friend Diana Clark, for seeing everything so clearly.

Divia Thani-Daswani, who deservedly sits atop the subcontinental media world. Thank you for reading, and rereading, and laying the bridge from where I am to where you are.

My thanks to my cousin Amrita Daswaney, who came along to that IPL match and sacrificed watching it to feed me ideas.

To the lovely and genteel Tulsi and Hari Chellaram, who throw Bombay's best brunches, and whose remarkable talent for pulling people together gave me fodder for this book and more.

And lastly, to my wise and perceptive friend, Naresh Thadani, for teaching me a thing or two about cricket, commerce and new beginnings.

Without all of you, my inner *Bombay Girl* would still be struggling to get out. Now, on to the next.